PRAISE FOR THE ___ MYSTERY SERIES

"Awesome."
"On the edge of my seat..."
"Page turner."
"I cannot tell you the last time a group of characters endeared me as quickly..."
"Diana Hunter is a strong, intelligent, and very likeable heroine."
"Grabbed me from the first page, and I sat up until 4:30 in the morning reading it."
"The story line is quick-paced and attention-holding. This one deserves 5+ stars."
"This book will keep you turning the pages to find out the who, what, why, and how."
"Couldn't put it down!"
"Left me wanting more."
"Peter and Diana have a great chemistry."
"I love the author's writing."
"A pleasure to read."
"Really captivating."
"Fast-paced, well-written, fun stories."

"I can't wait to read the next book in the series."
"I'm hooked."
"Kept me reading until the wee hours."
"Diana Hunter is becoming one of my favorite characters"
"Super read. Cracking heroine."
"One of the most enjoyable books I've read in a long time"
"A gem."
"Diana Hunter is knowledgeable, experienced, quick-witted, and even sexy."
"Can you write quicker, please?"

SNATCHED

BOOKS IN THE DIANA HUNTER MYSTERY SERIES

Hunted (Prequel)

Snatched

Stolen

Chopped

Exposed

Broken

COLLECTIONS

Books 1-3

Snatched

Stolen

Chopped

The characters and events portrayed in this book are fictitious. Any similarity to real persons, living or dead is coincidental and not intended by the author.
Text copyright © 2016 Alison Golden
All rights reserved.

No part of this book may be reproduced, stored in a retrieval system, or transmitted in any form or by any means, electronic, mechanical, photocopying, recording, or otherwise, without express written permission of the publisher.

Published by Mesa Verde Publishing
P.O. Box 1002
San Carlos, CA 94070

ISBN: 978-1517642907

"A book is a dream that you hold in your hand."

- Neil Gaiman -

SNATCHED

A. J. GOLDEN
GABRIELLA ZINNAS

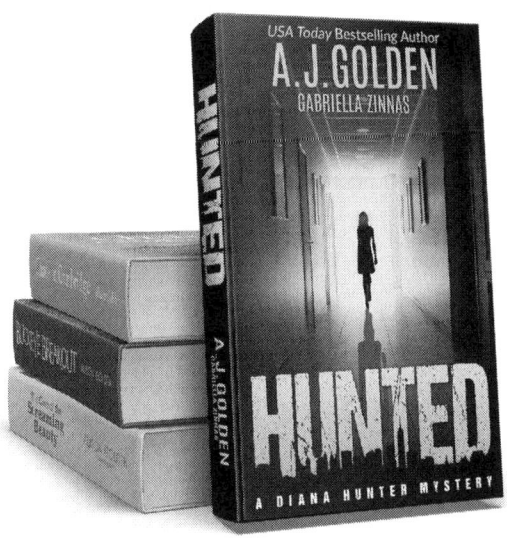

"Your emails seem to come on days when I need to read them because they are so upbeat."
- Linda W -

For a limited time, you can get the prequels for each of my series - *Chaos in Cambridge, Buckeye Breakout, Hunted* (exclusively for subscribers - not available anywhere else), and *The Case of the Screaming Beauty* - plus updates about new releases, promotions, and other Insider exclusives, by signing up for my mailing list at:

https://www.alisongolden.com/diana

CHAPTER ONE

I N ONE SMOOTH, swooping motion, Diana Hunter bent over. That's when she saw him. A man under a tree outside her apartment. Usually, she wouldn't have taken any notice. He looked engrossed in the book he was reading, and it wasn't unusual for people to sit by the ocean on the grassy lawn behind the beach.

Raising her arms above her head and clasping her hands, she stretched her muscles, leaning from side to side, enjoying the slight tension and release in her hips, her sides, her shoulders, and her hands. She'd pushed herself hard on her run today. It had felt glorious after being stuck behind her desk almost around the clock for the past seven days. With her hands on her hips, Diana sucked in deep breaths of the salty air. But something wasn't right.

It was 7 a.m. No matter how much one loved it, reading outside at this time was odd. Sure, it was beautiful in the early morning, but then Royal Bay Beach was gorgeous at any time of day. The sun sparkled off the deep blue water, the grass lush and green, and the smooth, pale sand simply called out for bare feet to disturb it.

Diana had spent many an afternoon enjoying a good book curled up under a maple tree or admiring the flowers and shrubs that dotted the promenade alongside the beach. But not so early in the morning that it was still quite chilly.

She'd first noticed the man when she'd started her run, almost an hour ago. And he hadn't moved an inch since then. Something was amiss.

"Sir? Are you feeling alright?" No response. Diana tried again, a little louder this time. "Sir?"

She walked over. The man was pale. His lips were blue. His chest wasn't moving. Diana reached out a hand and placed two fingers on his neck. His skin was clammy and cold. There was not even a flutter of a pulse. This man was dead.

The urge to shout was strong, but she suppressed it. "Breathe, Diana, breathe. Roll with it. You've seen dead bodies before. Get a grip." Diana looked up to see if anyone was around. The beach was deserted. She pulled out her phone and dialed 911.

"What is your emergency?" the dispatcher said as soon as the call connected.

"I'd like to report a body. At the beach." Diana cleared her throat. "Please send an ambulance and the police."

"A body . . . ?" The dispatcher's tone was disbelieving.

"Yes. The man isn't breathing. He's stiff and cold. He's dead." Confronted with the operator's officiousness, Diana's voice had risen an octave. She took a deep breath. "Please send someone."

The dispatcher was suddenly all business. "Tell me where you are, and I'll send units to your location."

"I'm on the promenade near Royal Bay Beach, close to Stanley Park."

"What is your name, caller?"

"Diana, Diana Hunter."

"Stay there, Ms. Hunter. The police will be five minutes."

"Thank you." Diana disconnected the call and looked down at the body again. What could have happened to him? Who was he? How did he die?

Part of her wanted to turn away and ignore the situation. This wasn't her fight. She had been looking forward to spending a quiet weekend at home catching up on chores. But questions nagged at her. With a sigh of defeat, she scrutinized the body, scanning it with a practiced eye.

One thing was certain. He hadn't been there last night. She'd got in after midnight and would have noticed someone sitting on the grass at that time.

Diana was tempted to stand up and move away, but her curiosity got the better of her. She took another quick look around and leaned in further. Pinching the man's shirt fabric between the tips of her nails, she pulled the shirt away from his skin. She peered inside, but before she could react, she heard sirens. The cops understandably got rather touchy about strangers getting too close to corpses lying out in the open, so Diana jumped up and took a few steps to stand at an appropriate distance.

An ambulance, a patrol unit, and an unmarked police car pulled up next to the curb. As the paramedics sauntered over, Diana watched the policemen get out of their patrol vehicle. One of them looked young. He was pasty and pinched. This was probably his first body. As Diana tried to hide a small smile, she felt a light touch on her elbow. A shiver of adrenaline rushed through her body like lightning.

"Are you Diana Hunter?"

"Yes."

"Ms. Hunter, I'm Detective Peter Hopkinson. Can you tell me what happened?"

CHAPTER TWO

DIANA GAVE THE man a quick once over. He wasn't exactly what she was expecting. In her experience, with a couple of exceptions, detectives were paunchy middle-aged men with perpetually irritated demeanors thanks to a lack of sleep, poor dietary habits, and even worse relationships. Her experience had never involved a man who looked like he'd stepped off the cover of *GQ* magazine. Peter Hopkinson wore a smart suit, his hair expertly cut and coiffed, shoes shiny and expensive. Even his stubble was short enough to be sexy.

Diana cleared her throat. "Well, I found a body." Great going, Diana. Really. Like he hadn't figured that out by himself.

"Yes, I think we've established that," Hopkinson said gently. "Could you be a little more specific?"

For some reason, his quiet disposition annoyed Diana. She wasn't in shock, and she didn't need to be coddled. She drew her shoulders back and, in a much stronger voice said. "I saw this man under the tree as I left for my run over an hour ago. On my return, he was still there, his position unchanged so I investigated.

"So, the body was here when you left on your run?" Hopkinson tapped out notes on his tablet. It was the first time Diana had seen a detective use anything other than a notepad.

"Yes, I told you. But, at the time, I didn't realize he was dead. I thought he was reading, though it did strike me as odd. It was pretty chilly this morning, and people rarely come out quite this early." Dammit, now she was babbling.

Hopkinson looked at her, narrowing his eyes, his lips pressed together in a thin line. "And what made you stop to *investigate* on your way back?" He raised his eyebrows and waited for her answer.

Diana gritted her teeth. "As I said, he hadn't moved at all from his earlier position. I wanted to check he was alright."

"You noticed he hadn't moved?" The detective seemed skeptical.

"Didn't I just say that?" Why did he keep asking her to repeat herself? Didn't he believe her?

"It's unusual for the general public to be that observant as they innocently go about their business." Hopkinson's condescending tone set Diana's teeth on edge.

"Innocently? You think I had something to do with this?"

"Of course not," the detective said calmly. "I'm simply establishing the facts."

Diana felt her temperature rise a degree. Dislike of Hopkinson crept through her like an icy mist as logic fought a battle with her feelings. She knew he needed to ask her these questions, but he was wasting her time. Not to mention, insulting her.

First, he treated her like a silly little woman, and now he was inferring that she might be involved in whatever terrible event had happened to the man whose corpse lay a few feet away. Male model looks or not, Diana had the sudden and overwhelming urge to tell the detective to shove it. Or slap him.

"Your tone implies something different. For your information, the facts are that there is a body drained of blood lying outside my building," she snapped. "However, it is complete fiction that I killed him, drained his blood into my bathtub, dragged him out here, let him sit around for a few hours, and then called the police on myself to deflect suspicion." She snapped her mouth closed in irritation.

"That's quite some imagination you've got there, Ms . . ." Hopkinson consulted his notes. "Hunter."

Diana clenched her teeth. She took a deep breath. He was right. She had posited a realistic scenario of what might have happened. A scenario that betrayed her. Except for one thing. "And just how exactly would I get a body that weighs at least 180 pounds down from my apartment, on my own, without leaving a trail of blood, and without being seen?"

"I don't know. Perhaps you could tell me." The detective watched her closely, his expression inscrutable.

"You're being serious. I can't believe this. I wish I'd never made the call. I should have simply walked on by."

"I'm sorry, Ms. Hunter, but all of this is a bit strange, especially considering how much you seem to know about the body and what might have happened." Great. She'd dropped herself in it, and now she had to extricate herself. Well, offense was the best form of defense . . .

"How much I know? What exactly are you suggesting?"

The detective stiffened. "Well, I would be quite interested to know how you know the body was drained of blood. A general member of the public doesn't typically know the signs."

The detective's tone was much colder than it had been before. Diana took a deep breath to calm herself. "I got up real close to make sure he was dead, and his color suggested he'd suffered severe blood loss." All dead bodies had the same waxen pallor whether or not they had lost blood, but she had to say something.

The detective cocked an eyebrow. "Is that the only reason you assume he was drained of blood?"

"Why else would I think that?" She hoped he was buying her response. She shouldn't have got close to the body. The last thing she needed was to be charged with obstruction or tampering with evidence and whatever else they would find to charge her with for interfering with dead bodies when she shouldn't.

"I don't know. Maybe because you killed him and are now trying to throw us off your trail?"

"You know, I was having such a nice morning."

"I can see how a body could ruin it."

"It wasn't the body that did it," Diana replied glaring. She could see Hopkinson's jaw working. Good. He was an ass.

"Is there anything else you'd like to tell me . . .?" Hopkinson's knuckles were white as he gripped his tablet.

"No, that's all."

"Very well. If you could come down to the station later on today so I can take your statement, I'd appreciate it."

"Didn't I just tell you what happened?" Diana knew it was proper procedure, but the fact that he wanted to go through what she had seen a *third* time was extremely irritating.

"As I'm sure you are well aware, it's just a formality. So, please, come to the station."

"No." How did he know she'd know it was just a formality?

"No?" Hopkinson stared at her as if she'd lost her mind. "What do you mean, no?"

"You want my statement, come to my place and get it." As soon as the words were out of her mouth Diana realized just how much like a proposition that sounded—especially when Hopkinson's pupils widened slightly. A blush crept across her cheeks. "I meant that this is the first weekend I've had some free time, and I want to catch up on chores. I need to get some vacuuming done. My fridge hasn't been restocked in ages, and everything is covered in dust." What was she saying? Could this day get any worse? "So, if you want that statement, I'll type it out, and you can pick it up later." She finished in a rush.

The detective didn't reply immediately. He regarded her carefully. "Yeah, sure. I'll pick it up later this afternoon." He was still giving Diana a weird look. What was it about this man and his highly attractive face that caused her to fly off the handle so easily?

"Okay." Diana rattled off her address and phone number, then turned to walk away. Hopkinson stopped her.

"By the way, Ms. Hunter, what was it you said you did for work?"

"I didn't. But I'm a magazine editor," she snapped.

He inclined his head, eyebrow cocked again. "That explains it."

"Explains what? Are you implying that my imagination has run away with me?"

He looked at her with a trace of surprise. "I didn't say anything of the sort."

"You didn't need to. I know your type."

"Wouldn't that be a case of the pot calling the kettle black?" he said. "Presumption."

Diana huffed in irritation. He had her. Deciding retreat was the better part of valor, she turned on her heel and marched toward her building, unable to resist throwing a parting shot over her shoulder. "Just to make your job easier, I'm pretty sure this was a body dump."

Dammit, again! Diana berated herself. Why couldn't she have kept her mouth shut? She didn't have any proof of it being a body dump. It might be the logical conclusion, given the location of the body and the wicked cut the man sported from sternum to navel. But still.

CHAPTER THREE

DIANA WALKED INTO her apartment, shutting the door behind her, and locking it firmly. Twice, she checked the lock was in place before pushing aside a coat hanging from a hook and placing her keys inside a box built into the wall.

As a reporter and magazine editor for a true crime publication, Diana interviewed some of the toughest characters in existence. She knew how the underworld worked, and it was ugly. The business model was simple, though; vulnerable, disadvantaged people were exploited by those with a sociopathic disregard for them. The victims didn't stand a chance.

Just recently she had written a feature on abused mothers and their children prostituting themselves to make money for food while pimps, hardened criminals, took advantage of them, out to make a buck. Throw in a few serial killers, and Diana had seen the worst of what the world had to offer, so she always locked her door. It might not stop someone especially determined, but it would give her an advantage if she ever needed it.

Just then, seemingly out of nowhere, a small cannonball of white fluff hurled itself at her, yipping and barking. Diana laughed as she got down on her knees, holding her arms open. "Maxie!" Max bounded up to her, licking her face, his tail wagging energetically from side to side.

Diana hugged him until he squirmed. She smiled down at the Maltese terrier, her constant companion and the love of her life. He always knew how to make her smile. Max sat down, still wagging his tail, his tongue hanging as he looked up at her expectantly.

"Alright, alright. Come on. Let's get breakfast." Diana walked into her stylish, modern kitchen. Red and black lacquered cabinets lined two walls, black granite countertops edged the perimeter, and an island, copper pots, and pans hanging above it, stood in the center.

Diana opened a cupboard door and pulled out dog food. She measured out the right amount and put Max's dog bowl down on the kitchen floor for him. Like a good boy, Max waited to be invited to dive in. "Eat, Max." In a flash, Max thrust his face into the bowl. Diana giggled and rolled her eyes. Typical male. As soon as food was present, Max completely forgot she existed.

Now that he had been taken care of, Diana walked into her bedroom. It was neat and featured the same modern lines and red and black color scheme as the rest of her apartment. A king-size bed with a black curved headboard, chrome accents, and inbuilt lighting dominated most of the space. Two small glass and chrome tables stood on either side of the bed. Red and black lacquered shelving units that held her makeup, some of her favorite books and magazines, and a single photograph in an ornate silver frame lined the wall facing her bed. Floor-to-ceiling mirrors hid her walk-in wardrobe.

Diana trailed her fingers over the photo frame with a small sigh. The photograph in it was one of her most cherished possessions. It was a shot of her parents. Whenever she saw it, her heart shuddered.

In the shot, her father gazed into her mother's eyes while she laughed at something he'd said. It perfectly encapsulated their relationship. As she looked at it, Diana ached to hear her mother's soothing voice and her father's deep and contagious chuckle. She yearned to be held by them, indeed by anyone, and to be told everything would be all right. She longed to be not so alone. But it was not to be.

Giving herself a mental shake and boxing the past into a section of her mind firmly out of reach, Diana shed her clothes. Dumping everything into her laundry hamper, she padded into the bathroom and turned the shower spray on, waiting for the water to heat while she counted to ten. She knew then that the water would be perfect.

As she showered, she thought back to the body and Detective Hopkinson. The detective had certainly looked better than the body, but the latter wasn't snarky or a know-it-all. Just who did that Hopkinson guy think he was? Insinuating that she was involved in the death, indeed. What a moron. Diana sighed. She was overreacting to the man.

Diana knew herself well enough to realize that her reaction had a lot to do with the fact that Peter Hopkinson was too attractive for his own good. Or for her peace of mind. And that she might have a wee chip on her shoulder concerning detectives who talked down to her. But she promised herself she'd be more careful when she next met him. Her instincts were good, and she wanted in on this case. She suspected the circumstances of it would make for a great article, perhaps even an exposé. And she was feverishly curious about why someone would leave a body on Royal Bay Beach right outside her home.

Diana turned off the water and stepped out of the shower. Drying herself with a fluffy white towel, she padded back into her bedroom and put on an I-have-chores-to-do outfit—a pair of yoga pants, a sports bra, and a tank top. She pulled her long, light brown hair into a ponytail and flicked her bangs from her eyes. They had gotten too long. She looked at herself in the mirror. "You need a haircut and your highlights refreshed, girlfriend."

Diana grabbed a cup of coffee and sat at her desk, a frosted glass and chrome affair facing the floor-to-ceiling windows in the living room. The windows overlooked the bay, a beautiful view that Diana drank in daily.

Clicking her mouse, Diana brought her three-monitor computer setup to life. She would get that statement written before the know-it-all detective turned up on her doorstep. Then she could simply hand it to him and he would leave. That suited her perfectly. The less time she spent in his company, the better.

Diana glanced outside. Her balcony looked directly over the crime scene. Immediately distracted from her statement, she grinned. She walked outside and looked down. The area was now devoid of life.

Diana raised her eyebrows. That hadn't taken long. She'd have expected forensics to still be examining the site. Since when did VPD get so efficient? Only a cordon of yellow plastic tape with *Crime Scene* printed on it indicated anything unusual had happened.

Max, who'd been snoozing in one of his three beds, barreled into the room. He was in the mood to play. Diana got down on one knee and petted the fluffy bundle of irrepressible energy. "Not now, Max. Mommy has work to do." He looked up at her, pleading. He gave a little bark.

"This is emotional blackmail," Diana grumbled. "But I cannot submit to you, Max. I have to get a statement written. Later, we'll go play."

Diana returned to her computer with Max at her heels. She sighed and focused, wriggling and flexing her fingers like a pianist before a concert. Opening up her word processor, Diana began to type her recollections. Her fingers flew across the keyboard, her speed testimony to the thousands of hours she spent with it. She included as much as she could without explicitly stating she'd done the unthinkable and touched the body before the police arrived. While she worked, Max curled up beneath Diana's chair and waited patiently—sort of—occasionally licking and nipping at her heels until Diana's doorbell sounded.

Max shot off like a rocket to greet the visitor. He skidded to a stop on the shiny wood-paneled floor, almost crashing into the door, as he proceeded to bark as menacingly as he could. He was a tiny, white Maltese terrier. Menacing was not an adjective one could use to describe him.

Blowing out her cheeks, Diana rose from her desk. The visitor had to be Detective Hot-kinson. Jeez. She'd even come up with a nickname for the guy.

"Max, sit. Stay." Dutifully, Max sat. Diana schooled her features into a mask. She wanted this to be easy. She had to be nice she told herself. Welcoming. Then Detective Hopkinson would take her statement and be gone quickly.

Diana opened her door, a smile plastered across her face. "Hello, Detective," she said. Damn, he was as good-looking as he had been earlier. It hadn't been her overactive imagination. Bummer.

"Ms. Hunter," Peter Hopkinson replied, inclining his head.

CHAPTER FOUR

"**C**OME IN." DIANA stepped back from the door to make room for Peter Hopkinson and he swept past her with a grunt of thanks. Closing the door behind him, Diana took a deep breath to steel herself.

Max chose that moment to make himself known. This was his home, and other males were not welcome. The 6'2" detective was confronted with a yapping, growling ball of fur he could easily dispatch with a single, swift kick, but Max was undeterred. It was the first time a man had come onto his turf.

"Max, *no.*" Diana's words made no difference. Max refused to listen to her. He would defend his territory, and that was that.

Surprising her, Detective Hot-kinson bent down and sat on his haunches. "What have we here, eh?" He reached out a hand, palm down, and held it out without moving any closer to Max, who remained growling, baring his teeth. The detective didn't move, but maintained eye contact with the terrier, waiting. Max's growling abated minus a couple of token barks to let Hopkinson know he wasn't a complete sap dog. Max looked at the extended hand quizzically, tilting his head. He sniffed it. A moment later, he gave a final yip and pushed his head under Hopkinson's hand.

"Who's a good boy?" the detective murmured, cupping Max's face in his hand, following up with a good scritch under the dog's chin.

"Traitor," Diana muttered under her breath as Max's eyes closed in ecstasy. "Max, bed," she ordered. "Now." With a disappointed whine, Max turned and dragged himself into her bedroom.

"Nice dog."

"Thanks." There was a brief pause while Hopkinson waited to see if Diana would say more. When it became clear she had no intention of engaging in small talk, he continued. "So, can I get your statement now?"

The low timbre of his voice sent a shiver up her spine. No, no, no. She could not, would not, be attracted to this condescending jerk of a detective. Now that the distraction caused by Max had passed and there was nothing else to focus on, Diana found herself scrutinizing him. She found it fascinating that a sprinkling of short brown stubble covered his perfectly square jawline. And that his sharp, clear blue eyes looked at her so intently...

"Ms. Hunter?

Diana cleared her throat, blushing that she'd been caught staring like a schoolgirl. "Yes? Yes, of course." Her voice was breathy. Quickly, she cleared her throat. She was being ridiculous. He was a fool. "I have about a paragraph left to write. Do you want a cup of coffee while you wait?" Argh, what was she doing? Now she was prolonging his visit!

Peter Hopkinson watched her closely, assessing, tiny

lines appearing under his eyes as he decided whether to accept her offer. Another shiver skated up Diana's spine. She almost missed his nod of acceptance.

Diana walked into the kitchen, closing a door as she passed, and poured him a cup of coffee. She raised her voice. "Do you want milk and sugar?"

"I take it black, thanks." His low voice came from immediately behind her. Diana jumped, nearly spilling the coffee. Somehow, Peter Hopkinson materialized next to her. How had he done that without her noticing?

"Here," she said, shoving the cup at him. He took it, and just like in every cliché romance novel Diana would never admit to reading, their fingers came into contact. It was like touching a live wire. The shock raked through her body to her toes. "Um, I'll go finish that statement."

Diana sat at her computer. "Focus," she muttered quietly. Squaring her shoulders, she forced herself to concentrate on finishing the statement. The victim deserved justice, and she needed to do her part. She had to help if she could.

"You seem to have a perfect view of the crime scene from here. Did you see anything this morning that was out of the ordinary?"

Jesus. Did he do that all the time? Creep about without people noticing? Making them jump out of their skin?

Diana shook her head. "No, but then I don't hang out my window at such a ridiculously early hour, do I?" She grimaced. That had been a bit excessive. "Sorry," she said with a sigh. "I think finding a body first thing in the morning has thrown me slightly." *It has absolutely nothing to do with you.*

Hopkinson smiled gently. "It's okay. Don't worry about it."

Diana stared intently at her screen. His smile had thrown her for a loop. It hadn't been a devastating smile. There were no teeth or crinkling smile lines around his eyes, just some mild warmth. But it was enough to distract her.

With some effort, she reviewed her finished statement. Finding a passage that read awkwardly, she tapped a pen against her lips as she thought of how to rephrase it, aware that the detective was watching her.

"So, I'm guessing you'd like me to sign it."

Hopkinson nodded. "That would be great."

Diana scribbled her name on the paper, pulled out a manila envelope, and slid the statement inside it. She handed the envelope to him, making sure her fingers were well out of touching distance.

"I have a few other questions for you," Detective Hopkinson said. "If you don't mind."

"Fire away." Getting up from her computer, Diana moved to the couch, before realizing her decision was a poor one. Hopkinson towered over Diana when she was standing. Now, she would get a crick in her neck and he would have the power advantage. Rookie mistake, Diana. Come on, get with it. Thankfully, without being invited, he sat in the armchair opposite.

"The victim's name was Leonardo Perez. Did you know him?"

"No, that name doesn't sound familiar. And I'm sure I haven't seen him around here. I didn't recognize him at all."

"And you have no idea how he ended up under that tree?"

Diana rubbed the bridge of her nose. "This again? I already told you that I saw him like that this morning when I left for my run. He wasn't there last night. I got in late—past midnight—and noticed nothing unusual. I would have spotted a guy trying to read under a tree in the middle of the night. But I've explained all this in my statement."

Detective Hopkinson nodded. "I'm just double-checking."

Diana accepted his reply. "Was he from around here?" She couldn't help but be curious.

"I'm sorry, I can't discuss it." He looked apologetic. Sort of.

"Sure, I get it. No problem. Just wondering if I should bolt my doors and windows. Or hide from a psychotic killer?"

"You should always bolt your doors and windows. But no, there's no indication you have anything to worry about in terms of a madman."

CHAPTER FIVE

THEY FELL INTO awkward silence. Hopkinson, leaning on his elbows, glanced around. "You have a nice place. It's not what I expected."

Diana tried to see her living room from his point of view. Like the rest of her apartment, it was neat, spare, minimalist. A couch with a black frame and red cushions curved around one corner. A matching armchair sat next to it. An oval coffee table with a lacquered geometric stand and glass top separated the two.

On the opposite wall from the couch was a frosted glass and chrome media center that matched her desk. The rest of the room was dedicated to her work. Her desk stood in front of the windows, while a black bookcase stood off to the right. On the left, she had two low cabinets with red and black lacquered doors.

She looked at him curiously. "What were you expecting?"

Hopkinson looked nonplussed. "I'm not sure. I guess I expected something a little more . . . girly." He choked on the last word as if he'd realized halfway through that it might not have been the wisest thing to say.

Diana laughed. "Let me guess. You were expecting lots of pink, lace, and frills. Maybe even a doll collection?"

Hopkinson grinned. Now he was showing teeth, clear, white, and bright. The skin around his eyes crinkled. As Diana had suspected, he possessed a devastating smile. "You're right, the doll collection was the first thing I thought of."

"I don't know if I should be insulted."

"No, it's just that . . ." he trailed off. "I didn't know what to expect but this was not it."

"You didn't expect to like my taste?" Diana found it remarkable that he'd wondered what her place might be like. And he'd given it enough thought to formulate expectations.

"Honestly, no. But then, I wasn't expecting coffee, either." Was he apologizing? Showing some remorse for being an ass earlier?

"I slipped something into it," Diana replied sweetly.

Detective Hopkinson paled and looked down quickly at his cup. "I'm joking," Diana said, rolling her eyes.

Hopkinson let out a long breath. "Sorry, I think I've been doing this job for too long. I've become suspicious of everything and everyone. We have to be so careful."

Diana nodded. She felt a little guilty for teasing him. "I understand. I'm sorry."

Silence descended again, but it was slightly less awkward than before.

"Out of curiosity, why do you think he was moved here?" Hopkinson asked suddenly. "Why do you think it was a body dump?"

"Are you going to suggest I was involved again?"

Hopkinson chuckled. "I never thought you were. It was just funny to see you get so worked up."

"What?"

"You have to admit, things did look a bit suspicious."

"Really? How so?"

"Well, in my experience, which is quite extensive by this point, it's not every day that someone finds a body and is quite so calm about it. Plus, you seemed to know more than you should."

"Like?"

"Massive blood loss. How did you know that?"

Diana sighed. She was going to get into so much trouble. "I may have looked inside his shirt."

"Ah. So, it was the gaping wound that gave it away?"

Diana nodded. "And that's also why I think he was killed somewhere else." Hopkinson cocked his head, inviting her to continue.

"With a wound that big, he would have been bleeding. A lot. But there was no blood on the ground around him. So, where did it go? Last time I checked, there were no reports of vampires living in the Vancouver area. And even if a few are hanging around, they couldn't do that good a cleanup job."

Diana was babbling again. Vampires? Really? When she glanced at him though, Hopkinson was grinning.

"Good call," the detective said, nodding in approval. "Well, thank you for the coffee. And for only joking about slipping something into it." He grinned again. There were those teeth. And the eye crinkles. Devastating. "I have to get back to the precinct. Here's my card if you think of anything else."

Diana took it and acknowledged his thanks with a small,

tight-lipped smile. "Thanks for coming around to pick up my statement."

Closing the door behind him as he left, Diana took a deep breath. She heard the click of nails on the floorboards and turned to see Max scampering out of the bedroom. She bent to pick him up and buried her face in his fur, feeling the tickle of velvety softness against her skin. "Well, that was one interesting morning, Maxie. What do you think of him, huh? Huh?"

CHAPTER SIX

PETER HOPKINSON SAT at his desk on the third floor of the Vancouver Police Department building and pulled out Diana Hunter's statement. The woman was as curious as hell, so he was intrigued to read what she had written. Her statement was over a page long, and he wondered what she'd found to write so much about.

A few minutes later, Peter was frowning. Diana's statement read more like a forensics report. She had included every last little thing, including the shabbiness of the victim's clothes, the air temperature, and the humidity. Would she have performed an autopsy if he hadn't shown up?

Diana had irritated him with her smarter-than-everyone attitude and her grey eyes and haughty looks. There was something about her that disconcerted him. He'd sensed she'd gain the upper hand if he let her. It was why he'd questioned her story twice; three times if he counted the statement sitting on his desk. She was a magazine editor.

What the heck did she know about crime scenes and dead bodies? Judging by her statement, it would seem quite a lot.

Diana's requirement that he pick up her statement from her apartment had been unusual. He'd acquiesced because he'd been curious and wanted to understand more about her. He didn't seriously think she had anything to do with his case, but his instincts were on high alert. He didn't find her entirely trustworthy.

The detective had been on his guard but she'd been more pleasant than he expected. When she opened the door to him, he'd used every ounce of willpower to keep his eyes on her face. What was wrong with the woman, answering her door looking like that? Didn't she know gorgeous, single women living alone attracted unwholesome attention from the types of people he came into daily contact with? She needed to be careful. Thank goodness for the dog. It'd saved his blushes.

Peter looked over Diana's statement once more. Her observations were astute. In fact, they were more instructive than the forensics report he'd received. He'd have to go back to the scene to cross reference her observations with their findings. He might even have to meet her again.

He groaned and reached for his phone. "Doctor Riddle, it's Hopkinson. Do you have anything yet on the Perez case we brought in this morning?"

"Hello to you, too."

"Sorry, Doc."

The man huffed. "Never mind. Actually, I do have something for you. And you can come down here to get it."

Great. For all his experience, Peter never liked the morgue. He couldn't figure out why. He'd seen way worse in the field. Perhaps it was the smell. "I'll be right down, Doc."

A few minutes and an elevator ride later, Peter walked

into the morgue at Mercy General. The smell of industrial disinfectant assaulted his nostrils. His sense of disequilibrium only intensified when he saw the body lying on the table, the medical examiner leaning over it. Riddle's arms disappeared almost up to the elbows as he reached into the corpse and pulled out organs.

Peter prided himself on having a strong stomach. He'd been a member of the Canadian Special Forces. He'd deployed to more war zones than he could count. He'd seen death. He'd meted out death. But messing around with a man's guts? Peter struggled to stomach it.

"Doc?" he said, breathing in through his mouth. The body was giving off a unique perfume that was not wholly pleasant.

Doctor Riddle looked up. "Good, you're here."

"So what was it you wanted to tell me?"

"Come, I need to show you something." Riddle waved him over, his arms smeared with what Peter could only describe as "goo." He hesitated and Riddle, his wiry salt and pepper curls threatening to escape from beneath his paper cap, glanced up at him. "I don't have all day, man."

Peter stepped forward. He clenched his teeth and looked down. "What am I looking at, Doc?"

"This man has no kidneys or liver."

"Huh."

"His organs have been removed. And that's not the worst part."

"Someone killed him, took his kidneys and liver, and there's something worse?"

Riddle nodded. "The cuts were precise. They were made by someone with medical training. The victim wasn't dead when his organs were removed, however. I'm pretty sure he was conscious when they cut into him."

Peter felt bile rise in his throat. "What makes you think that?"

The medical examiner closed the body up, pulling the edges of the enormous wound together. "I can find no traces of anesthetic. And take a look at this incision. It starts rough, choppy, then becomes straight and smooth."

Peter nodded, not trusting himself to say anything. Doctor Riddle continued. "Part of the incision is surgical, but part of it looks like it's been done by someone whose hands were shaking or while the patient was moving or struggling. This part of the wound," Riddle pointed to the section that was cut cleanly, "was probably cut after he passed out or someone held him down."

"Jesus."

"Horrendous, eh?"

"Organ trafficking, you think?"

"Yup, it's the only explanation I can think of. Afterward, they let him bleed out."

"He didn't die from his liver and kidneys being removed?"

Riddle shook his head. "Without them, he might have lived for a few hours, maybe even a day, *if* he'd been patched up. But, they didn't bother. They just cut out what they needed and let him bleed to death. Utterly callous."

"So, he didn't die under that tree."

"No. They would have needed equipment and a sterile environment to perform the procedure. They couldn't risk the organs becoming contaminated. They would have been worthless. And the amount of blood this man lost as he bled out would have saturated the area."

"And the area in which he was found was clean. Organ trafficking? Wow." Peter stared down at the victim, his distaste forgotten as he processed the medical examiner's findings.

"It was a terrible way to go, that's for sure." Riddle pulled off his latex gloves and threw them in a can, his disgust apparent in the force with which he did it.

Peter had seen people blown apart by IEDs and gunned down in the streets. He'd been the first on the scene when people overdosed on whatever drug was popular that day. But this was a new level of cruelty even to him. Torture. It was grotesque.

He turned to leave. "Thanks, Doc. Let me have your report as soon as it's done."

Riddle stared at Peter. He was a small, wiry guy, weary from decades of dealing with the worst of what happened to people. "Peter, you have to catch these people. This is the first one we've found but . . ." Doctor Riddle trailed off.

Peter nodded. "I know. There'll be a gang at work. We might find other victims and even if there aren't any yet, there soon will be."

"I'd rather not see a body like this on my table again."

"I'll do everything I can to stop them, Doc. Promise."

CHAPTER SEVEN

IT WAS EARLY and Diana stood on her balcony with a steaming cup of coffee in her hands. She took a sip now and then as she looked out over the bay. Max was curled at her feet, snoring. It was too early in the morning for him, but he preferred being close to her. When she'd left her bedroom, he'd followed, choosing to resume his beauty sleep wherever Diana went.

As she listened to his sniffs and snuffles, Diana tried to take in the view; the horizon, the sparkling, jewel-green ocean dotted with boats, the clear blue sky reaching seemingly forever overhead. But the crime scene below acted like a magnet, drawing her attention away despite her best efforts.

She couldn't seem to ignore it. She knew she shouldn't get involved. She told herself she should stay as far away as possible from this case. But there was something about it that drew her like a child to an ice cream.

Diana thrived on mysteries. Problem-solving was her thing. She couldn't turn her back. An unanswered question set her mind alight. And in this case, she had so many questions.

Who was Leonardo Perez? Why had he been killed? Why had he been left outside her building? And what was with that cut from sternum to navel? It took gutting to a whole new level. Who would kill someone like that?

Diana groaned. "I'm not going down there, Max. I'm not." But the yellow tape had been removed, and the scene beckoned to her. She shook her head. "No." Determined, she went back inside to get her breakfast, Max hot on her heels.

Her mind still on the case, Diana laid out dog food for Max and assembled her chocolate granola and yogurt. She stood at the island eating, but not tasting, and soon wandered back to the balcony, breakfast bowl in hand. She glanced back down at the tree. It was still early enough that only a few people strolled on the beach. A woman sat on a bench, reading.

A battle ignited Diana's brain. It wasn't unusual for her. Logic and reason frequently fought her principles and passion.

Maybe she could take another quick look. She'd be doing her civic duty. Maybe the forensic team missed something. They'd worked so fast, they couldn't have been thorough. She wouldn't technically be poking her nose in. She'd just be helping.

Diana nodded to herself. Yes, it was the right thing to do. She was out the door before she finished her breakfast.

Diana strolled out of the elevator and smiled at Jimmy, the day doorman, before spotting an elderly woman hunched over a metal-framed walker standing outside the automatic doors.

"Good morning, Mrs. Latham," Diana said, as they opened.

"Good morning, Diana. Off for your run?" Mrs. Latham lived right across the hallway from Diana. She was a sweet old lady who didn't have any family around. Diana checked in on her from time to time.

"Not this morning, Mrs. Latham. Just a quick stroll."

Mrs. Latham leaned in conspiratorially. "Did you hear that they found a body right by that tree yesterday morning?" The apartment block grapevine was clearly working in its usual efficient manner. Mrs. Latham's apartment was on the other side of the building from Diana's, so she wouldn't have seen or heard anything, but news traveled fast. Especially that type of news.

"They're saying he had a huge gash on his chest. Probably something to do with drugs." Mrs. Latham pursed her lips disapprovingly. Apparently, the grapevine wasn't just efficient, it possessed the speed and detail of an information superhighway.

"Yes, I did hear about it, though I have no idea what happened." Diana was reluctant to admit she'd been the one to find the body. If she told Mrs. Latham that, it would be noon before she got away.

"I would have thought with you being a magazine editor, you'd know all about it." Mrs. Latham looked positively dejected.

Diana smiled. "Well, I promise to find out what I can and tell you all about it."

The woman's face lit up. "You're such a sweet girl. Thank you, Diana."

"I'm sorry, Mrs. Latham, but I have to go."

The old lady nodded with a big smile on her face. "I'll be waiting for news," she said with a wink. Diana laughed.

Within moments, Diana was walking up to the tree the body had been propped against. The beach was still relatively free of people, except for the woman on the bench. She seemed to be paying close attention to her magazine, though, so Diana ignored her and focused her attention on the tree and the surrounding patch of grass and dirt.

With a glance around to make sure she wasn't attracting too much attention, Diana sank to her knees. There was a small, dark smudge at the base of the tree. Could it be blood from the victim? Unlikely. He'd bled out before he got there. So, who's was it? It didn't look old, it was quite fresh.

As Diana circled the tree, a glint of sunlight by her feet caught her eye. A green and brown keycard lay camouflaged in the grass. Smoothly, Diana covered her hand with a tissue and slipped it into her shirt pocket. She looked around again. No one was paying her any attention.

She got down on all fours and proceeded with a fingertip search, looking for anything else that might have been overlooked. As she stared closely at the ground, square foot by square foot, a pair of smart brown men's shoes suddenly appeared in her field of vision.

Diana swallowed. She knew exactly to whom those shoes belonged. She took a moment and then raised her head slowly, taking in the entirety of Peter Hopkinson from feet to chest.

She'd considered him tall when she was standing. From her current position, he looked even more imposing. And when her gaze locked with his steely blue eyes, he didn't look happy.

"Busted," she whispered.

"What exactly do you think you are doing, Ms. Hunter?"

CHAPTER EIGHT

D IANA JUMPED TO her feet. "Enjoying the scenery." Her voice rose at the end of her sentence so that her words came out as a question. Diana berated herself again. Rookie. Again.

As Diana scurried to brush strands of brown hair from her face and wipe the backs of her hands against her cheeks, Hopkinson cocked an eyebrow, taking in the grass stains that now covered the knees of her pants. "Enjoying the scenery?"

He sounded aghast, disbelieving. But to her surprise, in the next second, he burst out laughing. He had a strong laugh. The deep rumble teased the corners of her mouth, tempting them to rise and join in.

"Okay, I guess I could have come up with a more original excuse," she said.

"I think even walking your turtle would have been better," Hopkinson replied, still chuckling.

"Well, I wasn't expecting you to show up, now was I?" she admonished.

"Please accept my apologies. Next time I want to check

over one of my crime scenes, I'll call you in first to ask for permission." He was still smiling. So, he was joking, not being an ass.

"Apology accepted, and it's only polite to ask for permission." She winked. He smiled. Devastatingly.

Suddenly, remembering why they were there in the first place, they sobered. A man had died in a gruesome, diabolical way.

"Did you find anything?" Hopkinson asked, his tone brisk.

Diana nodded. "I think so. See here?" She lowered herself to her haunches, indicating the spot on the tree. "I'm assuming this is blood."

Hopkinson crouched beside her to get a better look. He pulled his phone from his pocket and swiped the screen a couple of times to magnify the mark. "I think you're right."

"But I have a question. I'm sure the forensics team has photos to place the body accurately, but if I remember correctly, this would have been behind the body, right?" Hopkinson nodded. "So whose blood is it?"

"Why assume it's not his? You have no idea how the body was handled. Maybe he was dropped and his blood spattered the tree with blood."

"Then there'd be more of it on the ground and over a larger area around the tree. And besides, he was dressed in several layers and virtually bloodless. He didn't have enough blood in him to spatter. The blood on the tree is likely someone else's, perhaps someone connected to the case." Diana looked at Hopkinson expectantly, waiting for him to agree with her.

Hopkinson nodded slowly, pursing his lips and turning down the corners, his chin wrinkling as he weighed up Diana's words. She was right that the blood was probably someone else's, but how did she know so much? Women like her didn't usually know about blood spatters, nor did they care to. But this one was positively energized. "Tell me more."

Diana growled. "Don't you see? If he was killed somewhere else, by the time they brought him here, he'd already bled out. If he'd still been bleeding when he was dumped, we'd have seen more evidence of blood. At least a few directional drops as he was carried. But there's nothing anywhere except for that spot on the bark." She indicated the area around them, which was completely pristine. Not a drop of blood in sight.

"Now," she continued without pausing, "I'm pretty sure whoever carried him here wouldn't have had their hands or other body parts covered in his blood as it would have drawn too much attention. But, it stands to reason that this is the blood of one of the people who put him here. Maybe they nicked themselves when they leaned him against the tree, or maybe they were involved in whatever was done to him and they got injured without realizing it. It doesn't matter. I'm certain it's not the victim's blood, and as an important piece of forensics, it should be tested."

Diana took a deep breath and looked at Hopkinson. He stared at her, dumbfounded. She'd done it again. Why did she never stop to think about how her theories sounded to others? To her, it was simply a matter of logic. To other people? Well, most had the same reaction as the detective. They didn't understand how her mind worked or how she knew what she knew, so they mistrusted her. It had happened many times and she never learned the lesson. She was compelled to share her ideas. Occasionally, someone would support her, and lift her up. Other times she got the same suspicious look the detective was wearing now.

"You know what? Forget it," she snapped. Hopkinson's eyes widened. "Just forget it," she repeated. She got to her feet and stomped off in the direction of her apartment. The detective called after her, but she ignored him. And then she remembered. Damn! She turned around and stalked back.

"I also found this," she said, her tone curt. She pulled the card from her pocket with the tissue. "I found this in the grass." She glanced at it. "And it looks like a keycard from a hotel about two blocks from here. I recognize the address."

"For God's sake, do I really need to explain the basic concept of contaminating evidence? You should know that just from watching TV shows," Hopkinson barked. "What possessed you to even touch it? You should have called me right away." He put on a latex glove and took the keycard from her. He dropped it into an evidence bag.

"No, you don't need to explain, but let me remind you that it was your forensics team that missed it. They did a terrible job of covering the scene. I was just trying to help."

Hopkinson shook his head and took a deep breath. "So, where did you find it?"

"Over there," Diana said, pointing to a spot on the ground. She wasn't feeling all that forthcoming anymore.

"Do you have any more theories to share with me?"

"I think I'm all theory-ed out for now."

"Or evidence, perhaps?

"No."

"Okay, then. Thank you, Ms. Hunter." Hopkinson looked at her evenly.

"I'll let you get on with your . . ." Diana waved her hand around, "*investigation.*"

"You make it sound like an insult."

Diana's eyes widened. "I'm sorry, I have no idea what you're talking about."

"Really?" Hopkinson stared at her for a moment before his face relaxed. "Fine. Have it your way," he said mildly. Diana turned to leave again. "Are you completely sure," he interrupted, stopping her mid-turn, "you didn't happen to find anything else?"

Diana's temper frayed. "If I had, I would have told you," she snapped.

"Really?" he said again. Diana's temperature ratcheted up another degree.

"Really," she said.

"So, you're absolutely sure you haven't found anything else and you don't know anything more about this . . . situation."

Blood roared in Diana's ears. She ground her teeth so tight they ached. Her eyelid twitched. Her hands curled into fists by her sides. She took a deep breath.

"Well?" Hopkinson prompted. His condescension wiped out all of Diana's good intentions.

"You pompous ass!" she shouted.

"What did you say?"

"You heard me. You are a pompous, ungrateful ass!"

CHAPTER NINE

"ALL I'VE DONE is try to help you, and what do I get in return? You dismiss me, patronize me, criticize me, and suspect me. Hell, I wouldn't have cared. It's not as if it's the first time this has happened. But I draw the line at having my integrity questioned." Diana was furious.

"Stop shouting, you insane woman." Hopkinson wasn't far off shouting himself. "What do you expect? You seem to know so much about what's going on, yet you claim no involvement. You find things the forensics team missed and have plausible theories galore yet you profess to be an ordinary member of the public with no specialist knowledge. Your damned conclusions are as good as any seasoned detective, but you claim to be a magazine editor. What the hell am I supposed to believe?"

"Maybe that I possess more than two neurons and I know how to use them? You're the detective! Use your brain! If I was involved, why the hell would I give you all this information? Wouldn't it be logical for me to completely derail your investigation instead of helping you?"

"How do I know you're helping me? Maybe you're trying to slow me down while your accomplices clean up the real crime scene. Maybe this time tomorrow, you'll be in the Cayman Islands, sunning yourself on the beach, enjoying the proceeds of your murderous, organ trafficking run." Hopkinson ran a hand through his hair, disheveling the style he'd crisply combed and gelled it into. "Damn! I shouldn't have told you that."

Diana's mouth fell open. "Organ trafficking?" She paled. She didn't know what shocked her more. That organ trafficking was taking place in Vancouver or that the detective thought her capable of something as heinous as being involved. "You think I'm capable of doing something like that?"

Briefly, Hopkinson's blue eyes shone with passion, then dulled. Diana noticed the confusion in them. His shoulders relaxed. "I don't know," he admitted softly. "I've experienced a lot of things. I'm not surprised by much anymore."

"Well, that's your problem, not mine." Diana's tone was glacial. "You know what? Get on with your investigation. Pretend you never met me. And I hope, for your sake, that you catch these people before we're knee-deep in bodies missing their organs." Diana turned on her heel and marched away.

Diana didn't look back as she stalked over to her building. Only once she was safely in the elevator did she crumble. Tears fell. Her eyes ached, her head pounded, but it was her disappointment that overwhelmed her. For some reason, she hoped Hopkinson would be different. But he was just like everyone else she came into contact with. A judgmental, ignorant bonehead.

Hastily brushing away the tears as the elevator doors opened, she walked down the corridor and let herself into her apartment, slamming the door behind her so hard that Max woke up and started barking. When he realized Diana was home, he quieted. She smiled softly and sat on the floor cuddling him. "Sorry, Max. Did I scare you?" Max licked her hand and put his front paws on her shoulders so that he could reach her face.

"At least you love me, right, Max? You'll always love me. And you'll never think me capable of killing someone to steal their organs, right?" Max whined and licked her face again. Diana smiled. Then she sighed. She shook her head at her own stupidity but the fact was that she couldn't let this case slide. It had nothing to do with her, but a man had died. If she could help to bring his killer to justice, then she had to do it.

Diana clambered to her feet and walked out onto her balcony. She glanced at the crime scene to see that Hopkinson was still there. He sat on his haunches in front of the tree and pulled a knife and an evidence bag from his back pocket. Diana watched him as he cut off a piece of bark and bagged it. So, he was going to get it analyzed, after all. Good call.

Before she turned to go back inside, Diana noticed that the woman reading on the bench was still there. "That must be one heck of an interesting magazine, don't you think, Max? I wonder if she heard my argument with the bad policeman? Let's hope not, eh?"

Diana looked at the woman again. She was stocky with short, fair, curly hair. She wore a T-shirt and cargo pants with tennis shoes. Nothing about her stood out, except that her magazine was so absorbing it had captured her attention for over an hour. Diana was a magazine editor. She knew that the average time a person spent reading a magazine was fourteen minutes.

After a quick shower to rid herself of the layer of grime that settled on her skin during her foray crawling around outside, Diana grabbed another cup of coffee. She eyed the chocolate bar she kept for emergencies but decided against it. This wasn't a chocolate situation. At least not yet. Instead, she walked into the living room and fired up her computer. It was time to get to work. But first . . .

She opened up a file marked *DB_Royal_Bay*, ignoring the lengthy list of other files in the folder that all started with DB but featured different locations and dates. She read through the file, made a few notes, and closed it.

Diana navigated to another folder and opened up an article she had been editing. It wasn't long before she was engrossed in her task. An hour later, she saved her changes and stretched her arms over her head with a satisfied smile. Now, she could relax and turn her attention back to the body by the beach. She checked the time. It was time for lunch.

Her doorbell rang as she stared into her fridge. Who could that be? She rarely had visitors. She didn't wonder for long. Max immediately yipped and scratched at the door. It could only be one person.

But Diana was not in the mood for another argument. She could pretend she wasn't there.

"Diana, I know you're home. Open up!" Peter Hopkinson banged hard on her door.

Diana? And how did he know she was home? "Diana, I know you're in there." He didn't let up.

Diana walked over to the door. "Go away! I don't want to talk to you," she said through the door.

"Please, open up," he said, quieter now.

"I'd rather not, thank you very much."

"We need to talk." There was a pause. "I need your help."

Diana snorted. "You should have thought of that before insulting me." She still hadn't opened the door.

"Look, this is ridiculous. Just let me in so we can talk. I went to the hotel and found the crime scene."

CHAPTER TEN

DIANA YANKED OPEN the door so fast, Peter nearly fell into her apartment. She bit her lip to hide her grin at the ungraceful way he caught himself on the jamb. That should teach him not to lean against other people's doors in future. She waved him in and closed the door behind him.

Max, ever the traitor, made a beeline for the detective. "Max, no. Bed!"

Hopkinson shook his head. "It's okay," he said with a smile. He scratched Max between his ears. Diana's dog was in heaven. And that's when Diana realized she was starting to hate Peter Hopkinson. One moment, she was arguing, ready to kill him or, at the very least, rearrange his face. The next moment, he was so gentle and cute. Ugh! He was driving her nuts.

Diana leaned against the doorframe, watching him. Hopkinson was a big man. And she had a small dog. He could easily pick Max up with one hand, but he was being so sweet. Diana's heart softened.

"I was just going to grab some lunch." Her words came

out low and husky. Quickly, Diana cleared her throat and pitched higher. "Do you want something?"

Hopkinson looked at her as he might a snake or a lion, his eyes assessing, calculating. Was she being serious with her offer of food? Or would she go ballistic again?

Diana huffed. "It's just an offer of food."

Hopkinson smiled sheepishly. "Sorry, I'm just not sure where I stand with you."

Diana shrugged a shoulder. "At the moment, you don't stand anywhere. I'm just offering you some lunch. Now, do you want something or not?"

"Sure, that would be great," the detective replied, frowning a little.

"What would you like?"

"Whatever you're having."

"Smoked salmon and cream cheese sandwiches with salad." She closed a door that was slightly ajar and sailed into the kitchen.

"Sounds amazing," Hopkinson said as he followed her. He removed his jacket and took a seat at the island, placing his tablet in front of him.

"Tell me how I can help you, Detective Hopkinson." Diana opened her fridge and took out the ingredients she needed.

"You know, I've never done this before, and I'm still not sure I'm doing the right thing now. I'm used to rules. I'm ex-military. Following the rules is in my blood. But this case . . ." Hopkinson paused. "Well, I need a fresh perspective."

Diana nodded. "I'll try," she said busying herself with the sandwiches.

Hopkinson watched Diana as she chopped vegetables for the salad. "Those are some serious knife skills you've got there," he said.

"I like to cook."

Hopkinson cocked an eyebrow. She was still chopping while staring straight at him. With a knife that could kill. Most other people would have chopped off a finger by now.

He let it slide, though. He wanted her thoughts on what he'd found out at the hotel more than he wanted to learn more about her ability to slice raw onion into transparent slivers while looking elsewhere. Diana breathed a small sigh of relief.

"So, you said you went to the hotel?" she prompted him.

"Yeah, and I found our crime scene."

She raised her knife, pointing the tip at him. "Hang on a second. Before I get back on this merry-go-round, we need to get one thing straight. If you accuse me of being involved in this one more time, even if it's just with a suspicious look, I swear I'll show you precisely how deadly a frying pan can be when I hit you with it."

Hopkinson let out a bark of laughter. "I promise, no funny looks or accusations. Although seeing you wield a frying pan might just be worth the risk."

Diana smiled and shook her head. She returned to her task. "So, I'm assuming the crime scene was a hotel room?"

Hopkinson nodded, his face serious again. "Exactly. The thing is that Riddle—that's the M.E.—found that the guy's kidneys and liver had been removed. He'd been left to bleed out."

Diana's knife paused for a fraction of a second. "Organ trafficking," she said. "I'm not surprised they took the kidneys."

"Why do you say that?"

"I did a story a while back about organ trafficking. I learned more than I ever wanted to know about how the black market for organs works. It's a huge and highly lucrative trade. It's active all over the world. And kidneys tend to be moved most often because they are the cheapest and easiest to get."

"How's that?"

"They don't have to kill anyone. We all have two kidneys and can survive just fine with only one. And a healthy liver will regenerate once part of it is removed and transplanted. Live donors for these types of transplants are used all the time, especially when a family member is a match. Then there's the transplant list if no live donor is available. The problem there though is the need to wait for a match. Sometimes, a patient will run out of time and then, if you are rich and unscrupulous, the option is to buy an organ on the black market."

"Go on."

"These rings often source organs from places like China and India, where they might pay upwards of $500 for something like a kidney. Doesn't seem like a lot of money for a body part, but these people are desperate. The donors are brought over, the surgery is performed, and the donor shipped home, with no one the wiser. The ring then sells the organs for tens or hundreds of thousands of dollars."

"But if they can do it like that without attracting attention to themselves, why kill this guy? It would draw down more heat than necessary. Plus they have a body to dispose of. I mean, we may never have learned of the activity if it hadn't been for the dead donor showing up practically on your doorstep."

"The only explanation I can come up with is that Mr. Perez is unique in some way. He must have had a very rare combination of blood and HLA typing."

"What's HLA typing?"

"It's a criteria used to match organ donors to recipients, along with blood type."

"So, you think Perez was the only suitable match for the buyer."

"Yes, he must have refused to donate willingly so they took the organs by force, killing him in the process." Diana tipped the vegetables from the cutting board into the bowl. "Or they planned to kill him from the outset. Clearly, compassion for the donor wasn't their top priority. I'll bet a crazy amount of money was paid for those organs because, as you said, this is an exceptionally high risk for an organ trafficking ring to be taking. They've exposed themselves. The money must have been worth it."

"Yikes. What a way to go."

Peter watched Diana as she dressed the salad and pulled out two plates and forks. She set the sandwiches and salad in the middle of the table and took a seat on the bar stool next to him. "Dig in."

"Thanks." Peter didn't need to be told twice. He reached over and grabbed a sandwich. He took a bite out of it and munched thoughtfully. "There's something I don't get. Riddle said that they didn't use anesthesia, that Perez was cut open while he was awake."

Diana's fork froze halfway to her mouth. "What?"

CHAPTER ELEVEN

"DOCTOR RIDDLE didn't find anything to indicate the presence of anesthetic and the shape of the cut led him to conclude Perez was awake and aware when the procedure started."

Diana took a bite out of her sandwich as she considered what he'd said. "There's something very bad going on here."

"I agree."

"What did you find in the hotel room?"

Peter rolled his shirt sleeves to the elbows and leaned forward. "It was almost completely spotless by the time I got there so I wasn't hopeful, but they forgot one thing." Diana rolled her eyes. Something so simple, yet so important.

"And so did the maid. I found a piece of blood-soaked gauze under the bed."

"Bingo! I'm guessing it was Perez's blood."

"I think so. I'm still waiting for the DNA results. Unlike what you see on TV, these things can take a few days."

"In a few days, these guys will have cleared out never to be heard of again," Diana said.

"Yeah, I know. And that's my problem. My hands are tied until I get the results from the lab. My superintendent doesn't want me going around asking questions until we're certain that the hotel really is the scene of the crime."

"So, he'd rather wait and risk these guys escaping?"

Peter nodded. "Politics," he said with a shrug.

"What does politics have to do with a bunch of thugs stealing people's organs before killing them like animals?"

"I have no idea. All I know is that the super told me to back off until I had proof that the hotel room was the scene of the crime."

"Very curious. I wonder . . ." Diana muttered to herself. "What was the name of the hotel again?"

"The Hazeldene Inn."

Diana stood but held up her hand when the detective made to follow her. "Stay here. Finish your lunch. I'll only be a moment."

Diana sat down at her computer and fired it up. She ran searches until she found what she was looking for. She printed off a report and took it back into the kitchen.

"Guess who has a controlling interest in the Hazeldene?"

Peter looked at her and then at the piece of paper, she'd slid in front of him. "Oh, great," he said with a groan.

"Mr. Barry D. Gutierrez. He's one of the richest men in Vancouver. He has several legitimate businesses but they only act as cover."

"He's suspected of having ties to every illegal activity in the city, from gun running and prostitution to drug distribution and human trafficking, but we've never been able to indict him. We've found more than a few witnesses face down in water after committing to testify against him and people are running scared. No one speaks out against him anymore. It's like he's covered in a slick of oil. Nothing ever sticks. No wonder the super told me to back off." Peter grunted.

"You think your superintendent is protecting him?"

Peter shook his head. "Donaldson? No way. He's been after Gutierrez for more years than I've been with VPD."

"Then why did he tie your hands like this?"

"Because I had a run-in with Gutierrez a while back, and I may have overstepped the mark slightly. Donaldson warned me that he'd have my badge if I ever went near Gutierrez again."

Diana hid a smile. Harassing Gutierrez sounded like something Detective Hot-kinson would do. "So, your superintendent is trying to protect you."

"Looks like," Peter said, drumming his fingers on the table in frustration. "But it's not doing my case any favors."

"You know, just because Gutierrez owns a stake in the hotel, it doesn't mean he's involved in this."

Peter snorted. "Gutierrez would gut his own mother if he thought he could make a buck."

Diana lifted a hand to stop him. "Listen for a sec. Gutierrez isn't stupid, as evidenced by the number of times he's gotten off and the fact that he isn't rotting in prison, right? So why would he get someone to perform an illegal procedure in one of his hotels and let the guy die? He would have known it would lead us directly to him."

Hopkinson laced his fingers on his head and pursed his lips. "You might be right, but it would be great if he'd made a mistake this time."

Diana shook her head. "I'm sorry, I can see you'd love to arrest him, but I don't think he's involved in this. He's not that stupid. What name was the room registered under?"

"Let's see." Hopkinson reached for his tablet. "Montclair."

Diana blinked. "Maybe the name is connected somehow," she said.

Hopkinson shook his head. "Unlikely. It's a common name. It was probably the first one they came up with."

Diana acknowledged his logic. He was right. It was a pretty common name.

"You know, in a situation like this, if I wanted to find out who was involved for a story I was writing, I would follow the money."

Peter glanced up with a wry look on his face. "I did think of that. But I have no idea where to start, remember? We don't know who the buyer is."

"But you have all the information you need already," she pointed out.

"How so?"

"Leonardo Perez. Get your M.E. to do a full work-up on him and work backward. Find out who he would be a match for."

Hopkinson's eyes widened. He nodded as thought through Diana's idea. "He's got rare markers. There can't be many people with the same. That's a great idea! I can run Perez's results against the national transplant wait list."

"The recipient must be on it. Most people don't sink to buying organs on the black market until the situation is dire."

Hopkinson jumped to his feet. "You, Ms. Hunter, are a genius," he said with a wide grin. "I have to go." He grabbed the remains of his sandwich and dashed to the front door. He waved. "Thank you."

Diana smiled and flicked her hand. "Go. Find the buyer." Hopkinson nodded and disappeared. There was a bang as he closed the front door. In the silence that followed, Diana found herself staring at its white panels. Her head full of thoughts, she struggled to shake them, and fifteen minutes later, as she swept the kitchen floor, it occurred to her that she'd cleaned up after lunch without remembering a thing about doing so.

CHAPTER TWELVE

HOPKINSON CALLED RIDDLE. "Doc, can I get a full work-up on Leonardo Perez?"

"What do you need it for?" Riddle was curt. He was like that. He didn't have patience for small talk and that suited Hopkinson just fine, especially today.

"I need to find out who he could be a possible organ match for," Hopkinson explained. "I'm wondering if he has rare markers that made him very attractive to someone who was perhaps running out of time to get a donor in the usual way.

"Ah, I see. Good idea. I'll get right on it. It will take a while, though."

"How long?"

"You can have the results first thing tomorrow. I can't do any better than that."

Peter sighed. "Okay, so be it." He ended the call and got in his car. Firing up his engine and pulling away from the curb, he was on autopilot.

Diana Hunter was unusual. It was rare that he came across someone who processed information or made connections on the fly like she did. The way her mind worked was uncommonly logical and quick. How did she know as much as she did? How had she honed her skills? And who the hell was she, really?

As his mind turned over, Peter became restless. He drummed his steering wheel with his fingers and started humming to settle himself. Hypervigilance had been drilled into him during military service, taken to a new level in war zones, and became his constant companion after his brother was killed five years ago. Matthew had been shot in the head execution-style, and the killer never found.

At the time, Peter had reviewed the circumstances with the detectives in charge of the case. The crime scene had been immaculate, every trace wiped away. The bullet was removed, so no ballistics match could be made. It had been a meticulously planned killing committed by someone who knew police procedure well. Since then, Peter had trouble trusting anyone, especially those who seemed to know more than they should. And he was having more than trouble trusting Diana Hunter. She *was* trouble.

What if he was kidding himself and she *was* involved in this organ trafficking case? That she was just playing the part of an innocent bystander? What if she was engaged in some elaborate game? He'd had the feeling since he met her that she was hiding something. And that feeling hadn't disappeared as he got to know her.

Each time he'd been in her apartment, there had been one room she'd seemed fixated upon. She acted like it was no big deal, but the life drained from her beautiful face when she realized the door to the room was open. She'd gone out of her way to ensure she shut it so he couldn't see inside. And, when he'd glanced over, he'd seen her stiffen.

Maybe she was hiding a body in there. She was hiding *something*.

Hopkinson parked outside his precinct and walked in. He would talk to his superintendent. He needed a second opinion on the whole situation. As he passed the bullpen silently and grim-faced, no one acknowledged him. Most of his colleagues knew him well enough not to disturb him when he was in a mood.

Superintendent Donaldson's door was open, but Peter still knocked. He stuck his head into the office. Donaldson looked up. "Can I have a word, sir?"

Donaldson waved him inside. Peter closed the door behind him and paused. Was he doing the right thing?

"Out with it," Donaldson barked. He was in his early fifties, with a distinguished field career behind him. Now he was in management and what came with the position didn't always sit well with the seasoned officer. Donaldson missed the chaos and unpredictability of being a street cop. Worse, he was loyal to his officers and had stuck his neck out for them once too often, angering his superiors. And somehow, the promotion to Chief that his reports knew he deserved, eluded him.

Peter drew a deep breath and took the plunge. He told his superintendent everything about Diana Hunter and what had happened since he'd met her.

"I just can't help the feeling that she's hiding something," Peter confessed. "I mean, it almost felt like she was the cop, not me. She's extraordinarily confident."

Donaldson scratched his chin. "We'll discuss the fact that you shared information with a member of the public later," he said, glaring. He leaned forward. "But is your beef with her that she's hiding something or you're just pissed that she's smarter than you?"

Peter stared, dumbfounded. Was he? The super might have a point. "Sir, I just want to close the case. And fast. Maybe she can help."

"But you say you suspect she's not being truthful."

"I don't know what it is. She seems helpful, knowledgeable, but something's not right. I get the feeling she's holding something back. I don't know, sir, maybe I'm just being paranoid."

Donaldson's glare bored into Peter. "What have I always told you?"

"Listen to my gut until it's proven wrong," Peter replied automatically.

"Precisely. Dig into the woman. Find out if she is who she says she is. Don't take her word on anything."

"Thanks, sir." He left Donaldson's office and headed to his desk and, more importantly, his computer. It was time to find out who Diana Hunter really was.

Peter spent the next two hours reading articles Diana had edited or written. She was a decent writer, writing on anything related to crime—individual cases, investigative techniques, outcomes. She seemed to have a particular bent for profiling. But nothing suggested anything other than a layman's interest coupled with some degree of training. There was nothing that marked Diana out as someone with a not-normal background. And that didn't calm Peter's nervous system one iota.

He shifted to a different tab and tapped in a password. He typed in Diana's name. "Bingo." A search result appeared. He'd found a file on her in their police database. He clicked and stared as a message appeared. He tried again.

A few minutes later, Peter contemplated his next move. Ms. Hunter *was* hiding something. Significant parts of her personnel file were classified. Every time he tried to access her data, he'd come up against the same wall. He picked up his phone and put a call through to his former military commanding officer.

Several phone calls and a lot of persuading later, Peter finally received his answer. At least, part of an answer. He knew why Diana's file was classified. Now, he had to decide what he should do next.

Diana apologized to Max. "I'm sorry, Maxie, I promise we'll go out a bit later. I can't take you where I'm going." Diana wanted another look at where she'd found Perez. Max would contaminate everything with his need to mark every tree and piece of dirt in his vicinity.

Diana suspected that someone deliberately left the hotel keycard in the grass for them to find. Maybe someone who had been forced into the trafficking scheme somehow. And maybe it was nothing, and she was getting ahead of herself. Whatever, she needed another look around.

Diana rode the elevator down, greeting Jimmy the doorman as she passed through the lobby. Walking over to the crime scene, she paced back and forth before getting down on all fours to crawl around. She brushed the scrub with her hand, sweeping from side to side until her hand hit something hard. It moved as she hit it. There was a rattle.

Diana peered through the undergrowth. A few inches away, she saw the dark red of a Swiss Army knife resembling a slick of blood among the grass, an empty key ring at one end. Diana reached out her hand but froze, remembering Detective Hopkinson's earlier scolding. She growled. She was going to have to call him.

As Diana reached for her phone, she saw her. The woman she had seen that morning. She was still sitting on the bench. And she was still holding the magazine. No one spent more than six hours sitting on a bench, reading one magazine.

Her instincts on high alert, Diana quickly grabbed the knife and got to her feet, brushing herself off. She made to walk to her apartment building. As she did so, the woman stood and headed in Diana's direction, cutting her exit off.

Diana immediately turned around and walked in the opposite direction. There was a coffee shop across the street, on the corner of the block. People knew her there. It would be difficult for anything to go down without witnesses. But before she managed more than a dozen steps, the woman caught up to her.

"So, did you find anything else, Ms. Hunter?"

CHAPTER THIRTEEN

UP CLOSE, DIANA realized the woman was much younger than she had thought. The woman couldn't have been older than thirty-five, but she had a look about her that suggested she had been through a lot in life, most of it unpleasant. The woman held Diana's gaze, her eyes wary, a cynical smirk crossing her lips.

"I'm sorry, I don't understand what you mean," Diana deflected. Better to act ignorant than give the game away.

The woman snorted and continued to smirk, her voice sickly sweet. "I think you know perfectly well what I mean, Ms. Hunter. I'm referring to the body that was discovered here yesterday. Leonardo Perez."

"Why would you think I have anything to do with that?" Diana asked. She had started walking again, forcing the woman to follow her. She was determined to get to that coffee shop.

"Come on, Ms. Hunter. It's okay. You can tell me. My name is Sergeant Brodeur. I'm working with Detective Hopkinson on this case."

"I see." Diana focused on the coffee shop sign. The woman must think her stupid. She had sat on the bench all morning. Had she been a member of Hopkinson's team, he would have said so. And she'd had lunch with him only half an hour ago.

"Can I see your ID?"

The woman ignored Diana's request. "Look, I'd like to go over some details we've uncovered about the case. Would you have a cup of coffee with me?" the woman asked, nodding in the direction of the coffee shop.

Diana stopped walking and scrutinized the woman, assessing her proposal. Opposing arguments battled one another in her head. She should politely refuse and high-tail it out of there. Her self-preservation instincts were screaming at her to do so.

But this woman was connected to Leonardo Perez's murder. She was digging for information about the case and seemingly impersonating a police officer while doing so. Diana had a golden opportunity to discover more about what was going on.

"Okay."

Diana and the woman walked into the coffee shop together. Diana waved at the baristas. They waved back. Jenny was taking orders today. Jenny had been her barista—if one could have a barista—ever since Diana had started coming in regularly. Jenny always went out of her way to make Diana's coffee special, even if it was just a more elaborate design in the milk foam of her drink.

Brodeur indicated an empty table in the corner of the crowded place. "Have a seat. I'll get the coffee."

Diana nodded and when the woman's back was turned, she slipped her phone out of her pocket. She took a quick picture of the woman as she stood at the counter and sent it to Hopkinson along with a message.

> Is this your Sergeant? Goes by name of Brodeur. Asking about Perez. At coffee shop around corner from my place.

Diana quickly hit send and, with a few taps and swipes, turned her phone into a recording device.

"Who were you talking to?" The woman walked up holding their coffees. She nodded at the phone and set their coffees on the table.

"No one. It was just an email from work about an article that needs to be published on Monday. They need my input on something."

Brodeur took a seat opposite Diana. "So, Leonardo Perez. What else did you find at the crime scene?"

Diana gave a small shrug. "I didn't find anything except the body." She hoped the woman hadn't noticed her pick up the Swiss Army knife.

"Then why were you nosing around the crime scene again today? Twice."

"Because I was curious," Diana replied with a shrug. "I'm a magazine editor. I used to be a reporter. It's in my nature to investigate."

"Maybe this time your curiosity has done more harm than good," Brodeur said. "Meddling doesn't become you."

"Does it not? Let me guess," Diana said, "you're going to throw the old cliché at me about how curiosity killed the cat, right?"

Brodeur stiffened. "Maybe. Sticking your nose in wasn't your smartest move." The woman's smirk had transformed into a snarl. Great, Diana had pissed off a woman with a gun hidden in a shoulder holster under her jacket. Diana noticed the bulge when the woman sat down. Genius, Diana, genius.

"Maybe not. But it's part of my charm." Diana smiled and held the woman's gaze over the rim of her coffee cup as she took a sip. Brodeur smiled back. But there was no comfort in the smile. Her eyes were hard, like chips of coal.

"So, tell me, how exactly did you find the body?"

Diana played along. If Brodeur was a police officer and working with Hopkinson, she would know.

Diana shrugged. "He was leaning against a tree. I asked him if he needed help, and that's when I realized he was dead. I called the police. That's it."

Brodeur cocked her head. "Ms. Hunter, you visited the scene twice more. Why did you do that?"

"Like I said, I'm a journalist. I was curious."

Brodeur rubbed her eyebrow. She sat back and folded her arms over her stomach. "I don't believe you. I'm getting the distinct impression you're not telling me the whole story."

"I'm sorry if that's the impression I'm giving. But that's all there is to it. I know finding a body should probably sound more exciting, but it's not. It's rather unpleasant." Diana wrinkled her nose.

Brodeur shook her head. "You must think I'm a fool, Ms. Hunter. I know Detective Hopkinson visited you twice at your home and that you were at the crime scene together this morning. And now I find you nosing around the same crime scene again. So, tell me, Ms. Hunter, if all you did was find the body, why are you still involved in this case?"

CHAPTER FOURTEEN

"I CAN ASSURE you, Sergeant Brodeur, that my interest is purely professional curiosity and I am not involved in this case. I'm just an unfortunate bystander who happened upon a murder victim, that's all. I could ask you something similar. Why are you asking me questions that I've already been asked by Detective Hopkinson? And answered, I might add. Several times." Diana was liking this situation less and less. She needed to do something about the Swiss Army knife in her bag. She needed to make sure it got to Hopkinson.

Brodeur leaned forward. "Listen—"

"You'll have to excuse me for a moment, Sergeant." Diana interrupted her. "I have to head to the ladies' room." Diana got to her feet. Brodeur drew her lips into a thin line, biting them. Diana quickly left the table before the woman could object and wound her way through the coffee shop to the bathroom.

Locking herself in one of the stalls, Diana paused the recording she had been making and dug the Swiss Army knife and a pen from her bag. She wrapped the knife in toilet tissue and addressed the package, swearing as she repeatedly tore the flimsy paper.

```
FAO: Detective Peter Hopkinson c/o
     Vancouver Police Department
```

Diana hid the package behind the toilet and pulled out her phone. She had a text from Hopkinson.

> That woman is not Vancouver PD. Do not engage. On my way!

Diana grimaced. It was too late for that. She typed out a quick reply.

> Found knife at scene. Left it in bathroom stall at coffee shop.

Almost immediately she received another text from Hopkinson.

> Give it to me yourself. Be there in 10.

Just as she was about to type out a reply, she heard a door swing. "Ms. Hunter, I think you've been in here long enough," Brodeur's silky yet threatening voice echoed around the room. Damn!

Diana put her phone back in her pocket and pressed the flush. She slipped out of the stall, making sure not to open the door too wide. She closed it quickly behind her.

"Sorry," she said. "I must have had something that didn't agree with my stomach and . . . Well, you get the idea." Brodeur wrinkled her nose with distaste.

Diana headed over to the sink and made a big spectacle of washing her hands. She put on far too much soap and created a rigmarole around washing it off as she stalled, hoping to give Hopkinson more time.

"Gosh, this is sudsy soap." She turned her back to Brodeur so the woman couldn't see her furiously rubbing her hands into a lather. Diana turned on the tap and let the water run without putting her hands under it. "It won't wash off." She rubbed her hands some more.

Brodeur cleared her throat. Diana glanced up, looking at the woman in the mirror. She was holding her jacket open. The grip of a gun peeked out from a holster that lay level with her ribcage. "Let's drop the pretense, Diana. You know I'm not a cop, and I know you have more information on this case than you're letting on."

Diana's muscles tensed. The two women were about the same size. The other hadn't drawn her gun yet. Diana had a chance. Perhaps she could make the soap she had on her hands work in her favor.

"Do just as I say. And if you try anything, I promise you I won't hesitate to put a bullet through the head of that pretty little barista out there." Diana threw Brodeur a frigid look. "Okay, lead the way."

"Oh no, Ms. Hunter. Please, after you. I insist." Diana clenched her jaw and stepped out of the ladies' room, her head held high. Brodeur followed closely behind. "Outside," she hissed.

Diana nodded. She was being kidnapped by a madwoman in the middle of the afternoon, with people milling around, and a detective a few minutes away. Amazing.

Diana followed Brodeur's instructions, unwilling to put Jenny at risk. They left the coffee shop and Diana spotted a black SUV with tinted windows parked just to the right, the back door open.

"Get in the car," Brodeur growled.

"Diana!" Diana and Brodeur froze. "Diana, you forgot your order!" It was Jenny. She stood on the sidewalk waving a bag and holding a cup of coffee.

Brodeur hissed in Diana's ear. "What's that about?"

"I get a chocolate muffin and a latté every day," Diana lied. "Jenny must have thought I forgot my order. If I don't pick it up, she'll know something is wrong."

Brodeur glanced back at the barista, unconvinced. "Go, but remember, you say anything, and I will put a bullet between her baby blues."

"I hate you."

Brodeur laughed. "Good."

Turning around, Diana walked over to Jenny, smiling. "Thank you so much, Jenny."

"Is everything alright?" the girl asked, looking at her worriedly. "It's not like you to order a drip coffee."

"Check the toilet stalls," Diana whispered. Jenny's eyes widened, but she didn't say anything. Diana grabbed the bag and latté and turned back to Brodeur.

Once Diana reached Brodeur's side, the woman plucked the coffee cup from her hands. "Can't have you wielding hot coffee, now can we? Someone might get burned. Get in the car."

Diana sat behind a man in the driver's seat. He wore a dark suit. The driver appeared short. He sat low in the seat. She couldn't see much of his face, but he wasn't well-built. Lines crisscrossed his cheek, and in the rearview mirror, Diana noticed his eyes were sunken. He looked frail.

But he had a gun, it lay on the center console, and she could tell from his eyes, that his smile was as predatory as Brodeur's. It didn't look like he'd ever visited a dentist in his life.

Brodeur slipped into the front passenger seat. She turned back to Diana, holding out her hand. "Phone!" she snapped.

"Excuse me?" Diana blinked.

Brodeur sighed. "Give me your phone, Ms. Hunter, or I'll ask Mr. Smith here to take it from you." The man in the driver's seat grinned wider, his yellow and black teeth revolting her. Diana handed her phone to Brodeur. The woman turned to the man. "Drive."

He put the car into gear and they tore away from the curb with such speed, Diana was thrown back against her seat. As they sped out of the city, Diana began to worry. They hadn't blindfolded her. They were letting her see where they were going.

That could only mean one of two things. Either they weren't planning on using the location they were taking her to for very long. Or, they planned to kill her.

CHAPTER FIFTEEN

WITH A SQUEAL of tires, Peter pulled up outside the coffee shop. He tore inside and looked around.

Jenny hurried up to him. "Are you Detective Hopkinson?" she asked. He nodded. "I'm Jenny Masterson," she said.

"I'm looking for Diana Hunter."

"Diana left this for you in one of the toilet stalls." Jenny handed Peter the package wrapped in toilet paper.

"Where is she?" he asked.

The girl wrung her hands. "She was with this other woman. They drove off in an SUV. It looked as if she was forced into it."

Blood drained from Peter's face. "Are you sure?"

"Yes. I called to her and tried to get her to tell me what was going on, but she just told me to check the toilet stalls, which is where I found that." She pointed to the object in Peter's hands.

"Did you get a license plate?"

Jenny looked stricken. "Oh no, how stupid am I? I'm so sorry, I didn't think to look."

Peter shook his head and held his palm up. "You did great. Really. Tell me about the car."

"I think it was a Chevy Suburban—black. It looked black. Or maybe it was dark blue. It seemed pretty new."

Peter's mind galloped ahead. What the hell had he done? He shouldn't have involved her. She was going to end up dead, and it would be his fault. He needed to order an APB on the car and the woman who had taken her.

"Can you tell me what the woman with Ms. Hunter looked like?"

"Well, she was about 5'5" or so. She had short, fair, curly hair and was sturdy, a bit overweight."

Peter took out his phone and scrolled to the photo Diana had sent him. "Is this the woman?"

Jenny nodded. "Yeah, that's her."

"Stay there a moment. I need to talk to you some more."

Peter turned away. He pulled up Donaldson's number and hit the dial button. "Sir? Look, I need the tech guys to trace Diana Hunter's phone pronto. She's the woman I was telling you about. It's to do with the organ trafficking case."

"Well, why are you calling me?" Donaldson asked suspiciously.

"I need you to make it a priority. I think she's been kidnapped and—"

"Kidnapped?"

Peter winced. "Yeah. She was seen being forced into an SUV. I've got a witness and a description of the vehicle. I've also got a photo of the woman who kidnapped her. It's not great—"

"What the hell! How did that happen? Get back here now."

"Yes, sir. What about the trace?"

Donaldson sighed audibly down the phone. "I'll get the tech boys to do it. You put out an APB on the woman and the vehicle. We'll talk about how this happened later."

Peter sighed. "Thanks, sir."

"And you better hope to hell we find the Hunter woman before something happens to her."

Peter made another call to order the APB before turning back to Jenny. "I need you to start at the beginning. You need to tell me everything you saw from the moment Diana walked into the moment she left."

"Well, when I saw Diana walk in, she wasn't alone, which struck me as pretty unusual. I mean, she's been coming here for years, but she's always by herself."

"Then what happened?"

"Diana sat at a table and the woman she was with came up and ordered two drip coffees. That was weird, too."

"How so?"

"Diana always orders the same thing. A skinny caramel macchiato with an extra shot of espresso, no cream. Except for her birthday. That's when she gets the full-fat version."

"What else?"

Jenny shrugged. "Diana's a regular. She comes in almost every weekday. She's always really nice and leaves a tip. We've become friends, sort of."

"Go on."

"Yeah, anyway, it was the order that got my alarm bells going. So, I kept watch. Diana seemed really uncomfortable while they talked. She headed to the bathroom, and after a few minutes, that woman followed her. When they came back, Diana looked angry but worried too.

"I didn't know what to do. I knew something was wrong. So, I grabbed a coffee sitting on the counter, threw a muffin in a bag, and ran outside, shouting her name, saying she'd forgotten her order. I mean, she hadn't. She never gets a muffin, but I just wanted to make sure she was okay."

"That was quick thinking. You did really well." Peter praised the girl, urging her on.

"Yeah, well, apparently I didn't do that great since she was still kidnapped."

"That's not your fault. You did much more than most people would have."

Jenny gave him a grateful smile. "Anyway, I called to her, and after the other woman said something, Diana came over. I asked if everything was okay. That's when she told me to check the toilet stalls. She said it quietly so no one could hear, then she grabbed the coffee and the muffin and went back to that woman, who pretty much pushed her into the SUV. Then they drove off like a bat out of hell." Jenny sucked in a deep breath. "Oh gosh, will Diana be alright? Please, find her."

Peter nodded grimly. "I'll do my best. Thank you. You've been a lot of help."

Turning on his heel, he left the coffee shop, pausing when he got to the sidewalk. He glanced around hoping to see surveillance cameras. There were none.

Peter's mind raced. How had he got in this position? What was he thinking involving a civilian in his case? Why hadn't he warned her off? Arrested and locked her up, even?

The thought of an innocent woman coming to harm because of his stupidity tied him up in knots. He got in the car, slammed his fist against the steering wheel, and roared.

His siren blaring, Peter tore the car away from the curb. All he could think of was Diana's smart mouth and how much trouble it would get her into. The people who had taken her were sadists, torturers, killers. They wouldn't spare her.

Ten minutes later, he parked in front of the precinct and marched straight into Donaldson's office. "We got anything, sir?"

The older man leveled a glare at him. "This is why we don't involve members of the public in police business. They cannot protect themselves. They aren't trained for this kind of work. What were you thinking?"

Peter cringed. He knew the super's assessment wasn't strictly accurate, but still. He'd messed up. All he could do now was fix things as best he could. "I don't know, sir," he admitted. He genuinely didn't know. She'd been so intelligent and helpful. He'd been drawn in.

But it hadn't been her place to get involved. He should have warned her off. Instead, he'd encouraged her. And, somewhere in the deep recesses of his brain, a thought stabbed at his consciousness demanding to be heard—perhaps he'd been swayed by those searching deep gray eyes . . .

"Well, obviously," Donaldson snapped. "They're trying to track her phone. Nothing so far. Same with the APB. What do you think their plan is?"

"I'm not sure. Hunter hasn't got any family in town. She doesn't have any family at all. Who are they going to contact?" Peter muttered.

"You're hoping for a ransom call?" Donaldson looked at him with surprise in his eyes.

Peter drew back his shoulders and took a deep breath. He needed to think straight. "Yes, they'll call. If they had simply wanted to kill her, they would have done so in her apartment. Or they could have taken her into the alley behind the coffee shop and shot her there. Instead, they impersonate a cop and kidnap her in front of witnesses. So, I'm assuming they want something."

"Impersonating a police officer? These people are bold."

"I wonder if they're desperate. That they're caught in a bind of their own making and are looking for an out. Look, I need some surveillance equipment, sir."

"What for?"

"I want to watch her apartment. In case someone shows up."

"Alright, you've got it, but don't think I've overlooked how your stupidity has contributed to this situation. We'll deal with that later."

Peter nodded. "Thank you, sir." He turned smartly and left the office.

CHAPTER SIXTEEN

"SO, THIS DETECTIVE Hopkinson is your knight in shining armor, is he?" Diana winced at Brodeur's saccharin tone.

"I have no idea what you're talking about." The woman was methodically working through Diana's phone.

"Well, he was the first person you texted when you thought you were in trouble."

"Only because you claimed to be working with him," Diana retorted.

Brodeur snorted. "You're more involved in the case than you let on. Of course, I knew that."

"Good for you. I'll give you a gold star when I'm no longer being driven around by two goons carrying guns. No offense."

The driver looked at her in the rearview mirror but only issued a confused "Huh?" Diana rolled her eyes. Clearly, he hadn't been hired for his intellectual capacity. Several beats too late, the driver laughed. "I like her."

Brodeur shot him a furious glare. "No one cares what you think."

The driver's face darkened. "Shut it, woman. Remember, we're both up to our necks in this," he growled. Brodeur said nothing further.

Listening with interest, Diana saw Brodeur pull out a phone from her pocket. She swiped and tapped Diana's phone screen and then checked her own. Satisfied, she opened the window and threw the phone onto the roadside.

"Hey!" Diana exclaimed. They were in the middle of nowhere, having left the city a while ago. Fields of crops surrounded them. She was never going to get her phone back.

"What?" Brodeur snapped.

"What did you do that for?"

"Why d'you think? I don't want anyone tracking us. Especially loverboy."

"But that was my phone!"

"Do you ever shut up?"

Diana clenched her jaw. A swift retort came to her lips, but she kept quiet. The last thing she wanted was to goad the woman into shooting her.

"That's better. Now, maybe we can finish our drive in peace," the woman said. "Unless, of course, you'd like Mr. Smith here to shut you up. Permanently." Diana remained quiet. "Thought not." Brodeur settled back into her seat.

Watching the scenery fly by, Diana's heart sank with every mile. The further they got from the city, the harder it would be to find her, especially now that her phone was gone. She thought of Leonardo Perez and swallowed hard. Isolated, captured, in the company of ruthless killers, Hopkinson was her only chance.

Peter skirted Diana's living room. He'd appreciated her minimalistic décor earlier. Now, it infuriated him. There was nowhere he could hide the camera that would give him a view of the room, her computer, and the entryway.

Max whined. Peter refused to make eye contact with him. The moment he'd walked into the apartment, Max had gone wild, snarling, barking, and even attempting to bite Peter. No man had ever entered the apartment without Diana being there. Max had eventually backed into a corner, emitting a continuous stream of low rumbling growls as Peter paced.

His eyes landed on the computer. The camera was small enough. He would put it on top of one of the monitors, one angled toward the door. Anyone would think it was part of the equipment.

After he set it up, Peter perched on his haunches and held out his hand. Slowly, Max scooted over to him and nudged it. "She'll be alright, little guy. She has to be. You'll see. We'll find her safe and sound." Peter got to his feet and walked into the kitchen, rummaging through the cupboards until he found a bag of dog food. He filled up Max's bowl and put it on the floor. Max walked over and sniffed at his food. He backed away without touching it and turned to gaze at the front door while letting out a pitiful whine.

Peter's jaw muscles worked as he contemplated what to do. His phone rang. It was Donaldson.

"Sir?" he said as soon as he picked up.

"Her phone has been found."

Peter's heart skipped a beat. "I'm guessing she wasn't found along with it?"

"No. It was at the roadside off Capilano Park Road in North Vancouver."

Damn! "Thanks, sir. I just finished setting up

surveillance in her apartment. I'm heading back to the precinct now."

"Good." Donaldson abruptly terminated the call.

"We're getting closer, boy," Peter said to Max. Finding Diana's phone wasn't much, but it was something. The detective looked into Max's deep brown, soulful eyes. He was tempted to take the terrier with him.

If kidnappers breached Diana's apartment, there was no knowing what they might do to her dog. Peter's involvement had already disturbed her life enough. The last thing he wanted was for Max to get hurt as well. His phone pinged.

Peter glanced at it. He let out a sigh of disappointment when he saw the text wasn't from Diana. And then he froze as he read the message.

> If you want to see Diana Hunter alive again, deliver $5 million as unaccompanied luggage to Vancouver International Airport. Leave the baggage stub and a ticket to Mexico City at the VanAM Airways airline counter. Otherwise, Hunter will be sold off as spare parts. You have until ten p.m. One minute late, and we start cutting her.

CHAPTER SEVENTEEN

PETER STARED AT his phone, then took a deep breath to calm himself down. In reality, this was good news. At least now they had a way of finding the people who had kidnapped Diana, a way of getting her back.

Peter looked down at Max. There was no need to take him after all. Filling Max's water bowl with fresh water, Peter was out the door in moments, slamming it shut such that it locked behind him. The old skills were the best. They never lost their value. On the way to his car, he placed another call.

"Hey, Pete," the person on the other end answered.

"Ryan, I need you to trace a number for me. I just got a ransom demand. I need to know where it came from."

Ryan Scott was a computer genius. He'd been a hacktivist until Peter arrested him as part of a larger case. At seventeen, Ryan faced a minimum of five years in prison, but Peter had seen something in him that he thought might benefit all parties or at least the law-abiding ones.

Peter convinced Donaldson that Ryan would be an

asset to their team. The super was reluctant but came around when Peter pointed out they'd never be able to afford someone with Ryan's level of technical skill. The super, with an ever-decreasing budget, could not deny Peter was right.

Ryan was less easily persuaded. He had been adamant that he'd rather go to jail than work for law enforcement. He held that view until Peter took him on a tour of a high-security corrections facility and they'd engaged in some long, sometimes fiery, coffee-fueled debates.

Eventually, Ryan understood that he could help more of his targeted constituency—those oppressed and disadvantaged—if he worked with the police than if he was against them. It had been three years since he made that decision. He enjoyed his work, even if it did sometimes feel like he had sold out.

Peter had complete confidence in Ryan. If anyone could trace where that ransom message had come from, it was him. "Send me the text and the number. I'll get right on it."

"Thanks, man."

"No worries." The line went dead. Peter quickly forwarded the message to Ryan and left him to get to work.

Peter got into his car and fired up the engine. He debated whether to call Donaldson or drive to the station to see him. He was only fifteen minutes away, but every second mattered. It was already four p.m. He made the call.

"What?" Donaldson answered.

"I got a message from the person who kidnapped Diana Hunter. They've demanded a ransom. I've already sent Ryan the text and number."

"What do they want?" Peter explained the contents of the message. "Well, that's just great, isn't it? Where are we supposed to get $5 million in less than six hours?"

"Sir, if it's unaccompanied luggage, they have no way of knowing if there's any money in it. Not before they let Diana go, anyway."

"Are you willing to risk it? How do you know the kidnapper doesn't have accomplices waiting to kill Hunter if the money isn't there?"

"Because I'm pretty sure the accomplices won't be in a helpful frame of mind. They're clearly desperate and the kidnapper only demanded one ticket," Peter pointed out heatedly. "If there are any accomplices, they'll be selling each other out quicker than a tray of hot doughnuts."

"Yeah, well, I'd rather be safe than sorry. Let me speak to the Deputy Chief Constable. We'll see what he says."

"Okay, sir. I'm on my way in."

When Peter got to the precinct, Ryan was waiting for him. "Sorry, man. It was a burner phone."

"Crap! What about the GPS? Any luck?"

Ryan shook his head. "Whoever it is, they know what they're doing. The GPS wasn't operational."

"Damn it."

"Hopkinson," Donaldson barked from his office, "get in here."

"Ryan tracked the message to a burner—"

"I know," Donaldson interrupted him. "DCC Burton has authorized me to buy a ticket to Mexico City. He's also letting us have $5 million."

"He is?" The DCC wasn't known for his largesse.

"Don't get too excited. Remember that case a couple of years ago with the counterfeiters?" Peter nodded. "The cash is still in the evidence locker. It's kept for situations such as this." Peter heaved a sigh of relief. "I've got to warn you, though, Burton's mightily pissed. I tried to cover for you, but there's only so much I can do."

"Thanks, sir." Peter was grateful. Burton was a vindictive tool who disliked Peter for some reason. Right now, though, Burton was his savior. Peter took a moment to say a silent prayer of thanks for the Deputy Chief Constable's decision.

"We still need to find out where Hunter is being held. We can't run the risk of the kidnapper pulling a fast one. I'd be a lot happier if we could get ERT involved. Better we get her out than we rely on the kidnappers playing ball."

"I'm on it, sir. We still might get a sighting of the car and I'll speak to forensics to see if they found anything."

"Fine. Go. If you get anywhere, let me know immediately. I'll put the ERT on standby just in case. Keep me in the loop."

"Yes, sir."

Peter ran up to the crime scene unit's lab. He needed their help and quickly. He knocked on the open door and stepped inside. "Tina?" Tina Xu looked up from her microscope.

"Hi, Peter. I'm glad you dropped by. I was about to call you."

"Do you have something?" Peter sounded desperate.

"I do." Tina swung around in her chair. She was slim and petite; her white lab coat drowned her. The sleeves were rolled up revealing white, delicate wrists. Her long dark hair had been pushed into a sterile cap.

"Let's start with the Swiss Army knife. Now, I don't have to tell you how I feel about evidence being tampered with, but luckily for us, Ms. Hunter's fingerprints were in the system so we could eliminate them. Unfortunately, other prints on the surface of the knife were compromised when she picked it up. But as you probably know, most people open a Swiss Army knife by pulling on the safety of the blade."

"You got a fingerprint, didn't you?" Peter breathed.

"Yup," Tina replied, popping the 'p'. "It's only a partial, but we got a match. It belongs to Dean Browning. He works as a registered nurse. Mercy General until recently. Now agency."

"A nurse? Huh."

"What's even more interesting is that Browning is currently in the private employ of Jonathan Abbott, who is extremely wealthy and currently on—"

"The national transplant waiting list, right?" Peter was getting excited. He finally had a real lead! "Tina, that's fantastic. You are a lifesaver!"

"I'm not done." Tina's brown eyes held Peter's blue ones.

"Oh?"

"We went over the hotel room with a fine-tooth comb, and while it was wiped pretty clean, we did find something interesting. Embedded in the carpet were traces of soil containing pesticides banned over a decade ago. We ran further soil analyses and tracked it to just one area—West Vancouver, relatively close to the Capilano River. Here, you can see it on this map." She pointed to her computer screen. "It's a well-trafficked hotel room so I can't guarantee this has any connection to your case, but it's possible."

Peter's mind spun. Maybe Diana was being held near the river. It was a big area, though. Or perhaps they'd taken her to one of Abbott's houses. Or maybe Abbot had a house near the river. And maybe this Dean Browning knew what was going on.

"Three leads. Wow. I have a lot of work to do. Thanks,

Tina." Peter rushed out and didn't stop running until he reached his desk.

He pulled up everything he could find on Jonathan Abbott. Tina had understated his wealth. He owned an array of businesses, many of which provided services to the oil industry.

"What's up?" It was Donaldson. Peter pushed his chair from his desk and looked up at his tall, heavy-set super. Donaldson sipped from a can as he listened.

"There was a fingerprint on the Swiss Army knife found at the scene of the body dump. It belongs to a nurse who works for one Jonathan Abbott. Abbot's unknown to us but happens to be as rich as sin. He's also on the transplant waiting list."

"Aha. So you think he ordered his organs instead of waiting?

"Yeah, that's what I'm thinking. He's got a rare HLA-type which matches Perez."

"A what?"

"H—, uh, it's like having a rare blood type."

"Okay, what else do we know about him?"

"He's in his mid-forties and been in the public eye almost his entire adult life, attending charity events and various galas, always with some model or starlet on his arm. But two years ago, he disappeared from view. There's been nothing on him in the press at all since then. There were rumors that he'd contracted some tropical disease, but nothing was confirmed.

"But then I found that he's been on the national transplant waiting list for the past eighteen months so whatever disease he developed must have affected his liver and kidneys."

"Sounds like it," Donaldson grunted. "So what are you thinking?

Peter's mind continued to work furiously. He analyzed every piece of evidence and information he had, connecting the dots. He cross-referenced the workup Riddle had done on Perez with what he could find about Jonathan Abbott. "I'm thinking that Jonathan Abbott might be the reason behind the murder of Leonardo Perez. Maybe we're not looking at traffickers that buy and sell organs at all. Maybe this is about one man, an extremely wealthy and powerful one, running out of time."

"But what about the Hunter woman? Where does she fit in?"

"I don't think the woman who kidnapped Diana is working for Abbott anymore. I think she's gone rogue. She's looking for another payday and a way out of the mess she's in."

"So you think that once he got his organs, Abbot cut this woman and her crew loose, pardon the pun. As it is, he must be in recovery somewhere having had the organs transplanted into him."

"He must have set up a private medical team and surgical operation to keep this all quiet."

"He would have the means to do that if he's as rich as you say he is."

"Right, I'm speculating, but I'm guessing the team that got the organs for Abbot have gone to ground."

"The fingerprint on the knife, whose was it?"

"A nurse by the name of Dean Browning. He worked at Mercy General until two months ago."

"Do you have an address for him?"

"Yep, he lives in Eastside."

"Get down there. Take ERT with you."

CHAPTER EIGHTEEN

BLACK CLAD, HELMETED, and masked, the men, not a scrap of their skin visible, scuttled like beetles to a front doorway in Vancouver's down-at-heel, crime-ridden Downtown Eastside. Peter stood at a distance, ready to follow them in as soon as they breached the threshold.

"Police! Open up!" One of the beetle men screamed. Behind him, two others held a battering ram as they readied to pulverize the door to gain access to the house. Another screamed order received no response, so they moved up and swung the ram. The sound of cracking, splintered wood briefly filled the air and within seconds, the dingy street emptied as the ERT moved inside.

Screams and shouts quickly followed. Peter rushed through the crumbling, dilapidated house. In a back room, an elderly woman raised her hands above her head, shouting furiously. She was sitting in a wheelchair surrounded by takeout boxes. A young child buried his face in her lap, his arms wrapped around her useless legs.

Another shout. Peter turned and leaped up the stairs

two at a time. In a bedroom, a barefoot man aged around thirty wearing a blue Hawaiian shirt and khaki shorts cowered in a corner surrounded by men armed with handguns and rifles. He was sweating, red-faced, and terrified. "Don't shoot! Don't shoot!" One of the men gave an order. The others evaporated like mist over a lake on a summer morning, leaving only Peter in the room with the distressed man.

"Dean Browning?" The man nodded and turned his face to the wall. Peter leaned forward and, hooking the man under his armpit, lifted him to his feet. He handcuffed him and led him down the stairs.

As they moved to the front door, there was a shout behind them. The woman in the wheelchair, alone now, said something in a language Peter didn't understand. "Don't worry, Ma. I'll be back soon," Peter's captive replied in English. There was movement to Peter's right. The young boy stood there, his huge brown eyes watching, wary, as he fidgeted with a toy firetruck. Peter shoved Dean Browning through the door to the waiting patrol car.

🌎

"I'm sorry, I'm sorry!" Dean Browning covered his face. He was still sweating, his knuckles dimples in the backs of his puffy hands. "I needed the money, okay? And I'm so, so sorry what happened to that man." Browning removed his hands and held Peter's indifferent gaze. "I had *no* idea what monsters I was getting involved with."

"Tell me more." Peter sat, unconvinced and uncompromising, with his arms folded. He'd seen this act plenty of times before. This one seemed genuine, though.

"They'll kill me."

"You're looking at life in jail as it is. And," Peter uncrossed his arms and lay them on the table, "it's the right thing to do. I think you want to do the right thing, don't you?"

Browning's eyes filled with tears. His fleshy chin wobbled. "It was so awful. I'm a nurse. I want to help people. This was so . . . callous. They had no idea what they were doing. They took what they wanted and just left him. I tried to do what I could, but they stopped me. Told me to get the organs to Mr. Abbott. That's what I was being paid for. When I got back, I was too late and not . . . enough."

"Who were they, these people?"

"I don't know. I'd never seen them before. I've been looking after Mr. Abbott for a year now. I work for an agency, more money. I was hired to be his nurse. I administer his meds, check his vitals, go with him to his doctor appointments, and help him with whatever personal needs he has. Everything was fine. It worked for me, anyway."

"What was he like as a patient?"

"Oh, you know. People who are sick aren't the happiest. Mr. Abbott is quite pleasant, an easy patient most of the time, but used to having everything his way. He could be a handful. He had a real difficult time having a health problem and not being able to throw money around to fix it, especially as his condition deteriorated."

"So how did you end up transporting a liver and a kidney on ice to him?"

"A doctor, not one of his regular ones, visited him and told me to go pick up a package. He told me not to tell anyone and that they would make it worth my while. He gave me an envelope full of cash and said I'd get double that if I did as I was told. There was 15,000 dollars in the envelope!"

"Was there anything else?"

"A keycard for the Hazeldene and a note that said '#323. 3:45 5/11.'

"Room number 323 at 3:45 on May 11th, right?"

Browning nodded. "I was told to take a cooler packed with ice with me and to tell no one." Browning sighed. "So you've seen where I live. I am the sole provider for my grandmother and nephew. They rely on me. I couldn't think of anything but what an extra $45,000 could do to our lives." Browning hit his forehead with his palm three times. "I'm so stupid, stupid, *stupid*."

Peter's hand shot out to grab Browning's wrist, bringing it down to the table where he gripped it. "Then what?"

"When I got there, it was chaos. This guy lay on the bed, unconscious, with a huge incision down his front. On the nightstand, on a dinner plate inside ziplock bags, were his liver and kidneys. There was blood everywhere!"

"How many people?"

"Three, two men and a woman. One of them was the surgeon, at least I think he was a surgeon. He was an older guy, maybe about seventy. He reeked of cigarettes. He was plugging the wound to stop the blood, but he was having no effect. The woman was on the phone, and the other guy ran around grabbing towels, blankets, anything to soak up the blood. There was *so* much blood." Browning looked away and wiped his upper lip with his hand. "I was in shock. The woman saw me, grabbed the cooler, tipped the organs into it, handed it back, and told me to go! I wasn't sure what to do and then the old guy pulled a gun on me. I hightailed it out of there."

"When I got to Mr. Abbotts, the earlier doctor was waiting for me. He was wearing scrubs. He didn't say a word, just took the cooler and turned his back on me to go into the house. I was completely dumbfounded."

"Did you know what was going on by this point?"

"Sure, I had guessed. But I had done what they wanted, and I hadn't got my money! I shouted at the guy, 'Where's my money?' He told me the woman in the hotel room had got it. I didn't know what to do. I certainly didn't want to go back there. It was like a scene from a horror movie!"

It occurred to Peter that there was no "like" about it, but he remained silent. "Did you go back?"

"To my eternal regret, yes."

"And?"

"The three of them were still there, but the guy on the bed was dead. When I came in the room they froze. The woman recovered quickest and this time, it was her who pulled a gun on me. She held me there, and I waited with the others until the early hours when she ordered me to help them carry the body down a back stairwell and into a van parked outside. That's when we dumped him under the tree by the beach. I just wanted my money and to get out of there. I felt like I was living a nightmare, but I was getting in deeper and deeper. I wanted to leave you clues without incriminating myself. I dropped the keycard and later, the knife in the hopes you'd find them. It wasn't much, I know, but I didn't know what else to do."

"Is this the woman in the hotel room?" Peter slid Brodeur's photo across the table to Browning.

"Yeah, that's her."

"What about the guy she was with?"

"Uh, I don't know him. He was older, like the doctor. Small."

"And the doctor?"

"No idea."

"Alright, look, someone will be in to build an e-fit from your description."

"What will happen to Nana and Jorge?"

"Uh, I'll get social services to drop in on them. Did you ever get the money they promised you?"

Browning shook his head sadly.

CHAPTER NINETEEN

THE CAR STOPPED. Brodeur got out and opened the passenger door. "Move over!" Diana slid across the back seat to give Brodeur room. Brodeur waved her gun. "Look over there." Diana did as she was told. What choice did she have? She twisted her head to look out at the dark, brooding, desolate landscape.

Blackness descended, and Diana's head jerked as Brodeur tied the blindfold behind her head. "What's the point of this? I can't see where we're going anyway." Diana huffed. Brodeur wrenched Diana's arms behind her back, and she heard the familiar rip of zip ties being fastened around her wrists.

"Do you ever stop talking? Shut up!" A whine and squeak told Diana that Brodeur had slipped along the leather seat. There was a bang as the woman slammed the door, and got into the front. The car's engine fired up. They were on their way again.

Diana strained to listen to sounds around her. Why had they put on the blindfold and zip ties? And what did it mean?

The car eased quietly to a stop so gentle brakes were barely needed. Diana estimated they'd been driving for two hours. The car door opened and a hand reached in to grip her upper arm and manhandle her from the car. A rough voice that Diana recognized as that of the old man driver told her to stand still. As she waited, the wind rustled through undergrowth. Low voices—Brodeur's and another man's—rumbled in the distance.

The voices stopped and Diana continued to wait patiently until she was violently shoved in the back. "Move!" It was Brodeur. Diana stepped forward, but stumbled on the rough ground, nearly toppling over. Brodeur swore and, catching Diana around the waist, half-carried her into a building. Immediately, Diana noticed that the temperature rose a couple of degrees, the wind stopped buffeting her, and the ground became smooth underfoot.

The reprieve was short-lived. Brodeur shoved Diana again, much harder this time. The force propelled Diana across the room. She crashed into a wall, smashing her chin against stonework, and sprawled to the floor.

"What the h—" Diana rolled onto her back and listened for signs of further attack. Footsteps tapped across the stone floor, followed by a door slamming. They were going to leave her alone for a while.

Diana continued to lay on the ground, conserving her energy. She was as vulnerable as a baby—sightless and without the use of her hands. Her chin throbbed. Her wrists were tied fast.

Something soft tickled her face, making Diana jerk away in surprise. Warm air rippled through the fine hairs on her jaw, and then something with the texture of coarse sandpaper swiped her cheek, making Diana pull away again. A tiny mewl told her that her companion was a cat.

Diana sighed with relief and wriggled into a sitting position. The cat climbed into her lap and mewled again. "I don't have anything for you, kitty. And I don't see how you can possibly help me," Diana murmured. Her thoughts strayed to Max. He'd be hungry by now. And anxious. She had to get out of there. But how?

She heard footsteps again, and the door opened. The cat fled.

"Gerrup." It was Brodeur's driver. Diana attempted to stand.

"I can't see. You've tied my hands. I need help," she said.

The old man growled as he leaned over to help Diana. His growl quickly changed to a howl of pain as his head flew violently backward. Diana hit the underside of his chin with her head and aimed her forehead at his throat. A second later, the man doubled over as Diana headbutted him in the stomach. As he recovered, Diana, still blind and helpless, ran in the direction of the door. But the man was too quick for her. He grabbed her around the waist and spun her to face him. Diana brought up her knee and kicked, but she was off balance and her kick was weak.

"You little—"

There was no hesitation. Again, a rush of air brushed the fine hairs of Diana's face, but this time it wasn't followed by the rasping tongue of a cat licking her cheek. It was followed by a man's closed fist connecting with the bridge of her nose.

Peter marched up to his desk, roughly shoved his chair aside, and leaned over his keyboard. Dean Browning hadn't given him anything specific that would lead to Diana and time was short. He only had four hours before he had to go to the airport with a bag of counterfeit money. Like Donaldson, he'd much prefer a rescue.

He pulled up a map of the area around the Capilano River that Tina Xu had shown him. Her phone had been found on the road out of Vancouver leading to Capilano Park. Would Diana's captors be using one of Abbott's properties to store her? Maybe a remote one, one off the beaten track? Peter knew he was doing a lot of speculating, but reasoned theories were his only option.

He researched buildings in the area indicated by Tina's soil analysis, looking for one that linked to Abbott. The area around Capilano River was mostly protected regional parkland so there were few privately owned properties on it. He found just nine.

Peter ran his finger down the list he'd pulled up on his computer. Named individuals owned eight of them, but none of them were Abbott. One, though, was owned by a shell corporation. The property, a farm, had been bought a little over a decade ago. Could that be the one he was looking for? No matter. It was all he had. Peter quickly printed off the information about the farm and Abbott and went to see Donaldson.

"Traces of soil from around Capilano River were found in the hotel room. There's a farm there owned by a shell company."

"Does it have links to Abbott?"

"It doesn't appear to have links to anyone, which is my point. Perhaps the owner wants to hide behind an anonymous shell corp. Maybe Abbott."

"You want to go haring off to a building that might have a connection to the case on the basis that it doesn't appear to have a connection with the case?" Donaldson demurred. "Your argument's too weak. I can't send an ERT into a situation so poorly defined. You need to dig deeper and find a connection."

"But, sir, we don't have time!"

"And I don't have the resources for a wild goose chase. Go do your due diligence."

Peter stormed from Donaldson's office. "Ryan!" Ryan's tousled head popped up out of a cubicle. "I need you to look into this shell corporation. I need to find out if there's any connection between it and Jonathan Abbott. And I need it yesterday!"

"Yes, boss." Ryan disappeared inside his cubicle as quickly as he'd appeared.

Peter grabbed his coat, his car keys, and the map of the Capilano River. He wasn't hanging around. He might not have Donaldson's agreement or backup, but he would investigate his hunch.

As he raced at breakneck speed through the streets of Vancouver, passing through the metropolitan district, then suburbia, and finally the open road, Peter worked on calming himself. He used all his elite military training to focus. His priority was to find Diana. He would find her, alive and unharmed, and together they would return to Vancouver.

Peter glanced at the clock on his dashboard. Two and a half hours until the airport deadline. His GPS told him he had two hours to his destination. He pressed his foot down further on the gas pedal and his speedometer rose by eight digits.

Peter turned off his lights a mile away from the farm and jumped out of his car. He checked the time. The journey had taken him ninety minutes. Jogging quietly, he kept to the roadside until he saw the buildings. Then, like a will 'o' the-wisp, he disappeared into the undergrowth.

Lights were on in the stone building. An SUV stood outside. Peter pulled a pair of binoculars from his jacket. The car was a Chevy Suburban, just like Jenny at the coffee shop had said. Peter pulled out his phone and sent the plate details to Ryan.

Crouching in the bush, Peter crawled closer. The silhouette of a man crossed in front of a lit window. The man gesticulated to someone out of sight. He seemed to be arguing. Peter's phone vibrated. Ryan had gotten back to him.

> Suburban is registered to Sunlink Inc. Abbott on board of directors. Also shell corp. is connected to an investment company owned by Abbot's brother-in-law.

Bingo! Perhaps Donaldson would see the light now. Peter checked his watch. It was 8 p.m. Two hours to go. There was just enough time.

Quickly, Peter tapped out a reply to Ryan and forwarded the text to Donaldson. Turning around, still keeping out of sight, he scurried back to his car.

"Alright, it lines up too well to be a complete shot in the dark, and we're running out of time," Donaldson said when Peter reached him. "I'll send the Emergency Response Team. Wait for them, you understand? No going in on your own."

"Yes, sir."

"That's an order, y'hear?" Donaldson repeated. "I know what you're like. I'll send a team to the airport. We'll apprehend the kidnapper when we get the word from you that Hunter is safe. If you don't find her, we'll apprehend this woman, anyway. Got it?"

There was no reply. Donaldson grimaced. He'd lost him. Talking to Peter was often like talking to an empty room.

CHAPTER TWENTY

THE ERT COMPRISED of eight men and one woman wearing black uniforms and protective gear. They were armed with shotguns, sniper rifles, and sidearms. They arrived in two armored vehicles and looked ready to fight a war. They stopped some distance from the farm and sent their coordinates to Peter. Within ten seconds he announced himself. He'd been waiting for them.

Peter had kept the farm under surveillance as he'd waited. He'd watched as the woman he recognized as Brodeur from Diana's photo had climbed in the Suburban and left. After he'd radioed the intel back to the precinct, Donaldson had sent a team to the airport to meet her. Satisfied that part of the operation was in hand, Peter refocused again. Diana's rescue was paramount. He was certain now she was inside the farmhouse.

Only Michael Stockton, the ERT team leader, got out of his vehicle to speak to Peter. "There's no way for us to approach without being seen. This land provides no cover." The moon and stars provided the only light. They'd shut the headlights off as soon as they'd turned off the main road. Stockton and Peter huddled at the roadside, discussing, before Stockton broke away and clambered into the back of one of the jeeps.

"We're going in low and quiet," Stockton told his team. "We don't know how trigger-happy this lot is. They might kill the hostage if we startle them."

"Wouldn't they want her alive so they could use her as leverage?" one of the women asked.

"That would be the intelligent thing to do, but we don't know who we're dealing with, and we don't know where the hostage is located so we'll have to go room to room. I'd rather not take the risk. Hopkinson will engage them first, so I want everyone close but down and out of sight, got it? Operate as rehearsed. Paramedics are on standby two miles away."

"Yes, sir," everyone replied, their voices in unison. One by one, they scrambled from the jeep. Stockton returned to Peter.

"There's a megaphone and a comms unit in the first jeep." Peter ran over to grab them. He had confidence in the ERT, at least as much as he had in anyone. These guys were serious. He wouldn't be surprised if they had a chopper tucked away somewhere close by.

"Okay, everyone, gear up, and let's head out."

Within moments, they were all crouching low to the ground and making their way toward the farmhouse. Stockton signaled for everyone to stop. Peter looked around. He didn't see anything or anyone. They'd all hit the ground, blending into the darkness. Good.

Stockton spoke into his radio, his voice sounding clearly in Hopkinson's earpiece. "Hopkinson, you're up."

Peter's voice rose into the cold, black sky. "This is the

police. You are surrounded. Come out with your hands on your head!"

There was no response. Peter caught a glimpse of someone pushing back blinds to peer out. He waited to see if the kidnappers would acknowledge him. Nothing.

"Seems they don't want to play nice," Stockton said. "Lynda. Johnny. Rob." The shrub rustled as three people began to move.

"Hopkinson, keep them busy."

Peter took a deep breath. "We are armed. We know you have a hostage." Through night vision goggles, he watched the three operatives circle the building and creep closer. Peter searched his mind for what else to say that wouldn't alarm the kidnappers but keep them focused on him for as long as possible.

"Your accomplice has abandoned you. She called in a $5 million ransom for the woman you're holding." He paused to let that sink in. "She picked up the money and a plane ticket at the airport. She was apprehended and is now under arrest," he lied.

There was more movement behind the blinds. Peter glanced over to Stockton, who nodded at him and then indicated the house. The sound of breaking glass reached him. Explosions followed and smoke billowed out of the broken windows. Grenades.

Seconds later, four men stumbled from the farmhouse. Protected by the remaining members of the team, Lynda, Johnny, and Rob broke cover to capture and detain them. It was easily done, the men coughing and choking.

Peter covered his mouth and nose with his shirt and led the team into the farmhouse. Methodically, they cleared each room. The house was large and had lain unused for a long time. A thick layer of dust covered everything.

Cobwebs hung from almost every surface. The few bits of furniture still in the house were old and broken.

One room was lived in. A half-eaten burger on the table had become dinner for a cat with missing clumps of fur. When Peter reached the room, the hideous thing had hissed at him. Fast food wrappers littered the floor. There was no sign of Diana and so he backed out of the room and tried the next door further along, at the end of a landing. And that's when he found her.

Blood drained from Peter's face. His heart rate plunged at the sight of her. Diana was unconscious, her skin pale and mottled. There was bruising around her wrists and ankles where she was restrained. A deep red and purple mark bloomed on her cheek. Her hair stuck to her forehead. She wore a hospital gown and was strapped to a table, barely breathing, the terrible air quality in the building affecting her not at all. She was corpse-like.

Peter gasped which half-choked him. He checked Diana for signs of life. Up close, he noticed the cut on her cheekbone and the skin around her left eye turning purple. A guttural sound left him, but, Diana was alive.

"Building is clear," Stockton said, reaching the room. "Paramedics are en route."

Looking down at Diana, Peter grimaced. He cut the straps holding her down. She looked so vulnerable. Nothing like the spitfire he had started getting used to.

Other members of the team would deal professionally with the person or people who had done this to Diana. Peter would leave them to it despite his urge to deal with them himself. He was already in enough trouble. Instead, he stood, silently waiting, standing vigil over Diana's inert body.

Eventually, after what seemed like an age, the ambulance arrived and the paramedics rushed in. Peter stepped back to let them attend to Diana. Her breathing was shallow, her heartbeat was weak. "Drugged with some superficial contusions. Unsure about internals. She should be okay, though," the lead paramedic reported.

It was time to call Donaldson. They could take Brodeur down.

CHAPTER TWENTY-ONE

DIANA REGAINED CONSCIOUSNESS slowly. Her eyelids were as heavy as dumbbells. When she did manage to open them, bright lights shot darts of agonizing pain through to the back of her head. She immediately closed them again.

"You're awake. Good. That's an excellent sign, Ms. Hunter. I'm Doctor Fraser, by the way." The young sandy-haired man in a white coat stood at her bedside, tablet in hand. Whatever happened to handwritten notes on clipboards?

Diana groaned. "Well, Doctor Fraser, can you tell me why I feel like a rhinoceros sat on my head?" Diana tried opening her eyes again, more slowly this time. The stabbing became a dull ache. Okay, she could live with that.

"You don't remember what happened? The kidnapping?"

"Oh." Memories came back, a trickle at first, then a flood.

"It's alright. You're safe now. The police rescued you. You're at Mount Sinai Hospital."

"My head." Diana groaned again. She didn't like hospitals. She hated them. "When can I go home?"

"Well, you were lucky. Other than a few bruises and a heavy dose of a drug that knocked you out cold, you seem to be fine. No concussion. No broken bones. We're hydrating you and I'll give you something for your headache." The doctor pointed to the drip connected to an IV in her arm. "You can start on light foods anytime. I'd like to keep you here another twenty-four hours for observation. Then, all being well, you can go home. Is there anyone you'd like us to call?"

Diana shook her head. "No, thanks." She paused for a moment. "I think it was the punch to the face that knocked me out. I don't remember being injected with anything."

Dr. Fraser sat in the chair next to Diana's hospital bed. He lowered his voice. "You have traces of Rohypnol in your blood. They probably administered it while you were unconscious. You must have been giving them a lot of trouble. Would you like me to bring in a social worker? You've been through a lot."

Diana shook her head. Pain exploded bomb-like inside her head. "Argh, no. No, thank you. How long have I been here?" she asked.

"You were brought in last night. Detective Hopkinson asked us to notify him as soon as you were awake and able to talk. I'll do that now, if I may. Or I can wait a little until you're feeling more like yourself?"

"It's fine. Thank you," Diana said softly. She closed her eyes. She'd rest a little more, and then she'd get out of there. Hopkinson would find her wherever she was. She drifted off to sleep.

Diana awoke with a start. She opened her eyes and lifted her head slowly. No pain. Good.

It was dark out. She must have been asleep for hours. Carefully, Diana pushed herself to a sitting position. Blooms of brightly-colored flowers frothed from a vase on her hospital table, a beacon of life amid a sterile, bland room. Reaching gingerly, Diana picked up the card that sat next to them along with her purse.

```
Sorry. Peter Hopkinson
```

Diana smiled gently. He was a man of few words, very few indeed, but they seemed heartfelt. He must have come to see her while she was asleep. The purse was a nice touch. He must have found it somewhere.

Diana glanced around. Now that she was more alert, the walls pressed in on her. Her heart quickened. She struggled to breathe. Diana needed out of the hospital, and she needed out now.

Carefully, she choked the drip administering saline into her arm and slipped the IV from her vein. She dressed as quickly as her shaky movements would allow, wincing every time the fabric rubbed against her chafed ankles and wrists.

Grabbing her purse, flowers, and the card, Diana peered out of her room. She looked right and left, checking the corridor for medical staff. Some officious nurse would shoo her back into bed if she was seen, and she didn't want that. The corridor was clear.

Diana walked out of the hospital, her head held high, trying her best to hide the pain. She didn't need anyone stopping her when she was moments from freedom. Once outside, Diana hailed a cab and she was away.

Half an hour later, Max's happy yipping greeted her as she walked into her apartment. She locked the door behind her and walked into the living room. Placing the flowers on the coffee table, she sank onto the couch with a deep sigh and patted her leg. "Come on, boy." Max wasn't usually allowed on the couch. He jumped up, licking her face until she giggled. She hugged him. "I missed you, boy," she whispered into his fur.

Diana looked around, gazing at her apartment. Her eyes landed on the photo of her and her father. She smiled. She felt terrible, but she was alive—cause for celebration!

Slowly, Diana pushed herself to stand and went into the kitchen. She pulled out the dog food. Her poor baby must be starving.

Diana reached to pick up Max's bowl and stopped. It was half-full. She never left food out for Max. He had a regular feeding schedule; his food doled out in exact quantities to keep him from turning into a barrel on legs.

Her thoughts elsewhere, Diana picked up a bottle of red wine before changing her mind. What else could she celebrate with? Chocolate! She pulled out the chocolate truffles she kept for special occasions and sighed with pleasure as she popped one into her mouth. Chocolate—one of the best ways to celebrate life.

Grabbing the box of truffles and a glass of water, Diana crept back to the living room and slowly lowered herself onto the couch. Picking up her remote control, she turned on some soft music and allowed herself to finally relax. She was home. She was alive. Life was good. She closed her eyes.

The doorbell woke her. Diana groaned. She refused to get up. She didn't have the strength. Perhaps, if she did nothing, they would go away. She waited quietly.

The lock rattled. The door creaked open. Ignoring the pain, her head throbbing, Diana turned to see who it was.

CHAPTER TWENTY-TWO

"HEY DETECTIVE," DIANA said softly. She smiled wanly.

"I think we've gotten to the point where we can use our first names, wouldn't you say?" Peter said as he walked into the living room. His hair stuck up and his stubble was longer than fashionable. He looked more than a little contrite. When he saw Peter, Max didn't move a muscle. He remained curled around Diana.

"I guess you rescuing me from the clutches of death gives you the right to call me Diana," she said with another small smile.

"Yeah, and you nearly dying to help me solve my case gives you the right to call me Peter. Jackass, too, probably." Peter grimaced as he studied her. "But I think we should stick to Peter."

Diana laughed softly. "Would you like some wine? I was thinking of having some."

Peter shook his head. "I'm driving. I just came to check on you. I heard you disappeared from the hospital, and I wanted to make sure you were okay. Should you be drinking? After what you've been through, I don't think it's a good idea."

"I doubt a glass of wine will kill me."

"I still don't think it's a good idea."

"Noted. Now, will you please sit down? You'll give me another headache. How did you get in, by the way?" She nodded toward the front door of her apartment. "I locked it."

"I'm a police officer. I know a few tricks of the trade," Peter replied.

"Huh." Diana thought back to Max's half-full bowl, the dog's muted response to the detective's arrival, the fact he wasn't desperate to go outside. She looked at Peter curiously.

Peter sat down and Diana noticed the dark circles under his eyes, the lines at the corners of his mouth. "I'm really very sorry," he whispered.

Diana looked at him. "It's not your fault. If anyone's to blame, it's that Brodeur woman."

"Georgina Dillon. That's her real name. Georgina Dillon. Or "Jo-Jo" as she's commonly known. She's got a rap sheet as long as your arm. Jonathan Abbott hired her and her goons to help him get some replacement organs."

Diana gasped. "Jonathan Abbott, the oil tycoon?"

"Why am I not surprised you know who he is," Peter said. He gave her a lopsided smile. "It turns out he got some tropical disease two years ago. It damaged his kidneys and liver to the point they couldn't do anything more for him. He's been living hooked up to machines ever since. He was on the transplant list but—"

"His typing made it difficult to find a match."

"Precisely. And, apparently, when you have so much

money and are knocking on death's door, your conscience can take a flying leap off the first cliff it can find."

"So, he decided to take matters into his own hands?"

"Pretty much. He hired Dillon and the others to procure Leonardo Perez for him."

"But who did the surgery?"

"A doctor who'd lost his license for engaging in unsafe practices. He took out the organs from Perez. And then a bought-and-paid-for transplant team put them into Abbott. Abbott should be thanking his lucky stars he's alive. Then again, he'll be going to prison for years, so maybe he won't."

"So they've transplanted the organs into him?"

"Yup, and he'd doing well. The surgery was considered a success."

"That's absolutely wild. He's alive and gets the 'opportunity' to experience prison because of organs transplanted into him from someone he murdered. I don't think he deserves to live," Diana said softly. "Having money doesn't entitle you to take someone else's life so you can live."

"Yeah, I get it. Dean Browning, a nurse, was the one who left the keycard, the blood on the tree, and the Swiss Army knife. He said he'd been paid a lot of money to transport Perez's kidney and part of his liver to the transplant team. He hadn't expected the organs to be removed without anesthetic or for the man to be left to die. Browning tried to leave us as many clues as he could."

"But why did they do it without anesthetic? It seems unnecessarily sadistic. And surely it made the organ removal more risky."

"No idea. Maybe they simply forgot it or they were in a big rush and panicked. Or just incompetent." Peter shrugged his shoulders. "Over the years, I've found the reasons for people's odd, seemingly inexplicable behaviors are rarely profound. They're usually mundane and ordinary."

"Ugh." Diana scrunched up her face and shivered.

"So, are you going to tell me what happened?" Peter asked.

Diana sighed. She quickly explained what had occurred from when Brodeur approached her to the moment she'd been punched, after which point she could remember nothing.

"He punched you? In the face?" Peter's low, controlled tone caused Diana to glance at him quickly. His jaw muscles had tightened, a vein pulsed on his forehead, and his fists clenched.

"Hey, I'm fine," she said softly.

Peter shook his head. "Sorry. Some things just make me see red."

Diana chuckled. "It was my own fault. I should have contained him but he took me by surprise. He was an old guy, and I didn't take him seriously enough. Rookie mistake. I did attempt to kick him in the balls."

"You only attempted?"

"He was a lot faster than I gave him credit for. And I was blindfolded and zipped."

"You could have castrated him verbally." Peter grinned.

"Thank you for the vote of confidence."

"Well, I have to get going. I have a mountain of paperwork to get through."

"Thank you for coming to check on me," Diana said, clambering to stand.

"Don't get up." Peter turned to look at Diana, his face pinched. "You shouldn't be thanking me. I shouldn't have gotten you involved."

"You didn't. I got myself involved. You underestimate

how determined I can be. I hate mysteries. I would have found a way to insert myself in this one, no matter what you'd said or done, trust me. It was a done deal from the moment I found the body."

"That's not the point. I should have found a way to stop you, and I definitely shouldn't have come here to discuss the case with you. But thank you for your help. Without it, cracking this case would have been a lot harder. Even if you did require a rescue requiring hours of manpower and thousands of dollars." Peter smiled again.

"My pleasure. Happy to keep Vancouver PD on its toes. And I'm quite certain you would have managed without me."

Peter shrugged. "Thanks anyway."

"Next time, though, try not to imply I'm the perp, okay? Like a red rag to a bull, it was."

"Next time? Who said anything about a next time? You are not coming within a mile of anything this dangerous again. I won't allow it."

Diana burst out laughing. "You won't allow it?"

"Look, I know you test out with a genius-level IQ and hold degrees in criminal psychology and forensic science, biotechnology, and computer science. You also have medical school training." Peter took a deep breath. "I also know that you worked for the Canadian Security Intelligence Service, and could probably investigate my cases better than I can. But I refuse to involve you like that again."

"If you know all that about me, then you know that it's not your call, right?"

"I don't care. You will not be working on any other cases with the Vancouver Police Department, officially or unofficially, if I have anything to say about it."

Without another word, Peter turned and stalked out of

her apartment. Diana watched him go. She gently squeezed Max. He hadn't left her side since she'd returned from the hospital.

"We'll see about that, won't we, Maxie?" Diana looked down at him and grinned. The kidnapping experience had been horrifying, but she'd enjoyed flexing her investigative muscles. And sparring with a certain detective. Diana popped another truffle into her mouth.

"After all, Max, we need to keep the good Detective Hot-kinson on his toes. Can't have him getting complacent, can we?" She would have to make a few calls.

Thank you for reading *Snatched*! I hope you love Diana as much as I do.

If you would like to receive the exclusive prequel to the Diana Hunter series, to learn Diana's backstory and what drives her so, as well as find out about new books and receive great bonuses, please sign up for my newsletter: https://www.alisongolden.com

After *Snatched*, the series continues with *Stolen*. After a seemingly impossible heist, Diana muscles in and kicks ass with the cops of VPD, including a certain Detective Peter "Hot-kinson."

Can Diana discover how the heist happened? How they were robbed, all at once... without anyone seeing a thing? Will Detective Hot-kinson allow her close enough to find out? Get your copy of Stolen from Amazon now! Stolen is FREE in Kindle Unlimited.

If you love the Diana Hunter series, you'll also love the Roxy Reinhardt mysteries. Will Roxy triumph after her life falls apart? She's fired from her job, her boyfriend dumps her, she's out of money. So, on a whim, she goes on the trip of a lifetime to New Orleans. There, she gets mixed up in a Mardi Gras murder. *Things were going to be fine. They were, weren't they?* Get the first in the series, Mardi Gras Madness from Amazon. Also FREE in Kindle Unlimited.

If you're looking for a detective series with twisty plots and characters that feel like friends, binge read the *USA Today* bestselling Inspector Graham series featuring a new and unusual detective with a phenomenal memory and a tragic past. The first in the series, *The Case of the Screaming Beauty* is available for purchase from Amazon and FREE in Kindle Unlimited.

And don't miss the sweet, funny *USA Today* bestselling Reverend Annabelle Dixon series featuring a madcap, lovable lady vicar whose passion for cake is matched only by her desire for justice. The first in the series, *Death at the*

Café is available for purchase from Amazon. Like all my books, *Death at the Café* is FREE in Kindle Unlimited.

I hugely appreciate your help in spreading the word about *Snatched*, including telling a friend. Reviews help readers find books! Please leave a review on your favorite book site.

Turn the page for an excerpt from the next book in the Diana Hunter series, *Stolen* . . .

USA TODAY BESTSELLING AUTHOR

A.J. GOLDEN

GABRIELLA ZINNAS

STOLEN

A DIANA HUNTER MYSTERY

STOLEN
PROLOGUE

THE STREET IN front of the Four Seasons Hotel was buzzing. A throng of people crowded around the red carpet leading to the entrance. Camera flashes exploded almost every second. Dozens of limousines queued up, waiting to let their occupants out.

As the long, black vehicles rolled to a stop, their back doors level with the strip of red that led inside the venue, valets swooped in to open the doors to allow Vancouver's élite to pour themselves out. , Dressed in their glittering, shimmering finery, wealthy business people, politicians, TV and film personalities collected themselves as they took their first steps toward the entrance, preparing for an evening of dancing and dining to support the British Columbia Children's Hospital.

Event planner Charlene Evans surveyed the scene. She led the team organizing the evening and was pleased to see it turning out so well. She watched men in tuxedos accompanying women in beautiful dresses and adorned with sparkling jewelry as they walked along the red carpet. The couples paused to have their pictures taken before crossing the lobby's marble floor, and entering the winter wonderland that the ballroom had been transformed into.

Ivory silk drapes hung from the ceiling. Snowy white tables and free-standing bars lit from within with blue lighting dotted the discothèque area. The dining room featured large, round tables with cream tablecloths and shiny gold plates. Chairs draped in white fabric added to the wintery, snowscape feel of the room. Newly arrived guests met staff carrying trays laden with glasses of champagne and hors d'oeuvres. Music played in the background and a stage was set up for a band to play later.

"I have to give it to you, Charlene. Everything looks amazing," said Neil Johnson, chairman of the BC Children's Hospital Foundation.

Charlene smiled. "Thanks. I'm glad all that hard work paid off. Now, let's hope it pays off a little more literally in donations."

"I'm sure it will. Who can say no to helping sick kids?"

Charlene laughed. "Well, even if they could, they won't because they all want the good publicity that comes from donating to a cause like yours."

"I'd accuse you of being cynical if you weren't completely correct," Neil said with a laugh. "Now, let's get out there and rustle up some money for the hospital."

A few hours later, after the six-course dinner had ended, the band played. Attendees made their way to the dance floor. Charlene picked up her glass and took a sip of champagne. She leaned into her neighbor, who was trying to tell her something. The room began to swim.

Charlene felt groggy. The disorientation was almost imperceptible at first, and she dismissed it. The dizziness was surely due to nerves and how frenetic she had been in the lead-up to the event. Perhaps the champagne . . .

But something wasn't quite right. Charlene could feel it. She put her hand up to her throat, suddenly instinctively disquieted. Her diamond necklace was gone; the diamond necklace loaned to her for the evening by a prominent jeweler. The necklace she had committed to wear in return for a hefty donation to the hospital...

Charlene's heart pounded. Exclamations of surprise rippled throughout the ballroom like an echo that, instead of getting fainter, got louder. One person after another cried out in astonishment and indignation. As the cries got louder, the music petered out with an out-of-tune jangle. Charlene looked around, her palms sweaty, her breathing picking up speed.

"My jewelry! It's all gone!" exclaimed one woman.

"My cash, too!" said a man. Guest after guest repeated similar sentiments.

"We've been robbed!"

"But how? When?" cried one woman.

Charlene couldn't believe it. She frantically looked at those around her. They *had* been robbed. But the woman was right. How? When?

"Someone call the police!" shouted a man. He was so red-faced that Charlene feared he would pass out.

When the operator answered her 911 call, Charlene explained there had been a robbery. How many thefts? Hundreds. How many robbers? She had no clue. Had it been a stickup? No, there had been no gunmen. Pickpockets? Maybe. She simply didn't know.

"I have three hundred guests missing all the jewelry, money, and other valuables with which they came into this ballroom three hours ago. I don't know how it happened, when it happened, or who did it. Please send someone."

Charlene trembled. Her voice had risen an octave. She

had never felt so violated in her entire life. It wasn't just that she had been robbed. It was that someone had got their hands on everyone's valuables *without anyone noticing a thing.*

To get your copy of *Stolen,* visit the link below:
https://www.alisongolden.com/stolen

"Your emails seem to come on days when I need to read them because they are so upbeat."
- Linda W -

For a limited time, you can get the prequels for each of my series - *Chaos in Cambridge, Buckeye Breakout, Hunted* (exclusively for subscribers - not available anywhere else), and *The Case of the Screaming Beauty* - plus updates about new releases, promotions, and other Insider exclusives, by signing up for my mailing list at:

https://www.alisongolden.com/diana

TAKE MY QUIZ

What kind of mystery reader are you? Take my thirty second quiz to find out!

https://www.alisongolden.com/quiz

BOOKS IN THE DIANA HUNTER MYSTERY SERIES

Hunted (Prequel)

Snatched

Stolen

Chopped

Exposed

Broken

COLLECTIONS

Books 1-3

Snatched

Stolen

Chopped

ALSO BY A. J. GOLDEN

As Alison Golden

FEATURING INSPECTOR DAVID GRAHAM

The Case of the Screaming Beauty (Prequel)

The Case of the Hidden Flame

The Case of the Fallen Hero

The Case of the Broken Doll

The Case of the Missing Letter

The Case of the Pretty Lady

The Case of the Forsaken Child

The Case of Sampson's Leap

The Case of the Uncommon Witness

The Case of the Body in the Block

FEATURING REVEREND ANNABELLE DIXON

Chaos in Cambridge (Prequel)

Death at the Café

Murder at the Mansion

Body in the Woods

Grave in the Garage

Horror in the Highlands

Killer at the Cult

Fireworks in France

Witches at the Wedding

FEATURING ROXY REINHARDT

Buckeye Breakout (Prequel)

Mardi Gras Madness

New Orleans Nightmare

Louisiana Lies

Cajun Catastrophe

All prequels are available as ebooks for free in my **Starter Library**. Sign-up here:

www.alisongolden.com.

ABOUT THE AUTHOR

Alison Golden is the *USA Today* bestselling author of the Inspector David Graham mysteries, a traditional British detective series, and two cozy mystery series featuring main characters Reverend Annabelle Dixon and Roxy Reinhardt. As A. J. Golden, she writes the Diana Hunter thriller series.

Alison was raised in Bedfordshire, England. Her aim is to write stories that are designed to entertain, amuse, and calm. Her approach is to combine creative ideas with excellent writing and edit, edit, edit. Alison's mission is simple: To write excellent books that have readers clamouring for more.

Alison is based in the San Francisco Bay Area with her husband and twin sons. She splits her time between London and San Francisco.

For up-to-date promotions and release dates of upcoming books, sign up for the latest news here: https://www.alisongolden.com/diana.

For more information:
www.alisongolden.com
alison@alisongolden.com

- facebook.com/alisongolden.books
- x.com/alisonjgolden
- instagram.com/alisonjgolden

THANK YOU

Thank you for taking the time to read *Snatched*. If you enjoyed it, please consider telling your friends or posting a short review. Word of mouth is an author's best friend and very much appreciated.
Thank you,

Printed in Great Britain
by Amazon